the viking

Blues

THE BENNETT'S BASTARDS SERIES

JENNIE KEW

He was her first love. She was his only.

Mia Caldwell knows how to get stuff done. Armed with a plan to transform her family home into a veteran's retreat, she employs the help of her childhood friend and former crush, Oliver Bennett. But banging the sexy blacksmith wasn't on her to-do list.

No longer an awkward teenage boy, Ollie is all man now with a successful business, a panty-melting smile and a body that would make Thor jealous. But he's not the only one who's changed. Mia isn't the same naïve teenager she was when she left Melville's Cross and she isn't afraid to go after whatever—or whomever—she wants.

Oliver Bennett knew from the first day they met: Mia Caldwell was the girl of his dreams. She was smart, funny and driven to succeed, not to mention she had a smile that could drop him to his knees and a dominant streak that could keep him where he fell.

All grown up and more commanding than ever, Mia still has the power to bend Ollie to her will, only this time he isn't holding back. He never told her how he felt way back when and it's not a mistake he's willing to repeat, but as their friendship turns a corner, can he convince Mia to give them the chance he knows they deserve, or is friends with benefits all they're destined to be…?

THE VIKING BLUES

Copyright © 2021 by Jennie Kew
Published by Wooden Key Press
Edited by Hot Tree Editing
Cover Design by Wooden Key Press
Character Art by Serene Yoshiko

ISBN: 978-0-9756117-4-6

2ND EDITION

FOREWORD

I think we can all agree that 2020 was a shit year, but what made it especially hard for me on a personal level was the death of my father, Bruce. He lived in a different state to me, and at the time of his passing, COVID-19 restrictions had closed the border between our states, meaning I couldn't even attend his memorial.

In the months since Dad died, I have struggled greatly with my anxiety, but have also had to deal with a host of other physical limitations. The arthritis in my spine has gotten worse, and I was diagnosed with severe osteoarthritis in my hips. These limitations have in turn only fed my anxiety, and have affected my ability to write my books the way I want to.

But, while they might be (temporarily) a little shorter than I or my characters would like, I am confident I can tell their stories with all the feelings, fun and fucking my readers have come to expect.

I hope you enjoy Ollie and Mia's journey in *The Viking Blues*, even if it is more of a day trip and less of an international long-haul.

I thank you all for your continued support.

Happy reading,

Jennie xx

Size Doesn't Matter – Heart Award 2024
Erotic Romance – Winner

Size Doesn't Matter – Passionate Plume Award 2024
BDSM Romance – Finalist

Size Doesn't Matter – Stiletto Award 2024
Erotic Romance – Winner

The Viking Blues – Heart Award 2021 (2022)
Erotic Romance – Winner

The Viking Blues – Passionate Plume Award 2022
Short Contemporary Romance – Finalist

The Viking Blues – Stiletto Award 2022
Erotic Romance – Finalist

His Own Heaven – Passionate Plume Award 2021
BDSM Romance – Winner

His Own Heaven – Stiletto Award 2021
Long Romance – Finalist

This Time Around – Koru Award of Excellence 2020
Short Romance – 2nd Place

This Time Around – Stiletto Award 2020
Mid-length Romance – Finalist

Third Time Lucky – Passionate Plume Award 2019
BDSM Romance – Finalist

Third Time Lucky – Stiletto Award 2019
Erotic/BDSM Romance – Finalist

"Be prepared to be taken along on a
wonderful, sexy, heartwarming, sometimes
tear inducing, slightly kinky joy ride!"
Review for *Third Time Lucky*

"This novel was so romantic!
I'm in love, love, love with Rafe! I will
read this book again it was so good!"
Review for *This Time Around*

"It's a sexy, sleek and highly addictive story."
Review for *His Own Heaven*

"Their story is heartfelt, sweet, deliciously
hot and sexy, romantic and more."
Review for *The Viking Blues*

"It joins the rest of the series on my keeper shelf."
Review for *Size Doesn't Matter*

For Bruce, forever sailing.

PROLOGUE

M elville's Cross, October, eighteen years ago.

Their chests rose and fell in unison like they were one living, breathing organism, and as they lay on their backs staring at the same spot on the ceiling above Ollie's bed, they slowly came to terms with what they'd done.

"So... that was sex," Ollie said, air heaving in and out of him. "I think I like it."

Beside him, Mia chuckled, causing the bed to bounce, and from the corner of his eye he saw her turn her head towards him, so he did the same. Turned his head until he was staring into her brilliant blue eyes and her sweet mouth was mere inches from his.

He longed for another taste of her—in more ways

than one—but he was smart enough to know he had to tread carefully in these untested waters.

The last thing he wanted was to scare her off with his need for her.

A need he'd felt for a very long time.

Even if she hadn't felt the same.

But maybe he'd been wrong about that?

Ollie still wasn't even sure what had happened, or how. They hadn't planned it. He certainly hadn't anticipated it. Hell, he'd had to steal a condom from one of his brothers, and he'd like to think he would have planned things out a little better had he known he was about to lose his virginity.

Mia had only come over to help him study for their final exams and yet somehow one thing had led to another and they'd ended up in bed, naked.

It had quickly become blindingly obvious neither one of them really knew what they were doing, but what they'd lacked in skill, they'd made up for with curiosity and enthusiasm.

"Did I hurt you," Mia asked, her grin softening into a shy smile as she lightly trailed her fingers over his cheek.

He arched one eyebrow. "I think I'm supposed to ask *you* that question, aren't I?" Then he got up to dispose of the condom.

"I meant when I pulled your hair?" she said, giving him a playful shove when he returned to the bed. "I pulled it pretty hard."

Ollie's nostrils flared and he licked his lips, leaned in closer. "I liked it," he said, quietly. "It felt... right."

She blushed but held his gaze, his fearless warrior woman. "Yeah, it did."

"Did you like what I did to you?" he asked, hating the uncertainty that laced his words.

"Which part?"

He rolled to his side and propped himself up on his elbow. "When I licked between your legs. Was that okay?"

Her grin returned as she mirrored his position. "It was better than okay. In fact, I wouldn't mind if you did it again."

"Again, huh?" He stroked his fingers over her hip, noticed her little shiver at his touch. "I thought we were supposed to be studying."

"Well," she hedged, trailing her fingertips over his bicep, "I'm pretty sure anatomy is on the final exam for Phys-ed."

"And knowing how to find the pleasure centre of a woman would be on the exam, right?" he said, sliding his hand farther down her leg, then dragging the limb over the top of his, bringing her pleasure centre flush against his.

"Obviously," she said, suddenly breathless. Her voice dipped into a husky growl that made Ollie's cock twitch with new life. "That's half our final grade right there."

Throbbing with need for her, he rolled her onto her back and tugged her slender leg around his waist. "I'd hate to fail because I hadn't studied hard enough."

"Speaking of hard," she murmured, rocking her hips

against his in a way that made his eyelids flutter and his body jerk to attention.

Attention he would willingly devote to their "studies".

Ollie surged forwards and stole a kiss, hard and quick. "I guess I should go steal another condom, then."

Mia ran her fingers through his hair, fisted them and pulled. His eyelids fluttered closed again and he groaned as the pain forced his lust higher, made his dick harder, the anticipation sweeter.

"Make it more than one," she whispered against his lips.

"As you wish," he whispered back, knowing he'd do anything for his girl.

Fulfil any request, follow wherever she led.

Ollie thought he'd known what it was to love Mia, but nothing had prepared him for the wealth of emotion he felt as he stared into her eyes and made love to her again and again on that sultry spring afternoon.

He gave her everything that day.

His heart.

His soul.

He would love her forever.

If she let him.

1

M*elville's Cross, January, present day.*

Oliver Bennett smiled, and the woman sitting opposite him held her breath.

It was a common reaction, and one he knew how to elicit with little effort. As the second youngest of nine siblings, Ollie had grown up learning to read body language, learning to listen, and realising what people didn't say was sometimes just as important, if not more, than what they did.

Leaning towards him with her arms spread open on the table, her head tilted slightly to one side, her cheeks flushed, and her eyes slightly downcast so she could look up at him from under her thick, luxurious and obviously fake eyelashes, her body language practically screamed

"Yes, I *am* a sure thing." And after releasing the breath he was sure even she hadn't realised she'd been holding, she gulped down a lungful of air, causing her breasts to rise and fall in a way designed to attract his attention.

And attract his attention they did.

Creamy flesh swelled above the low-cut neckline of her tight red T-shirt, and a slow appreciative perusal revealed two perfectly pebbled nipples poking against the soft-looking cotton. Oliver could well imagine how they'd feel in his hands and taste on his tongue as he laved them with attention. Oh yeah, he was a boob man, and breasts—especially a pair as nice as....

Shit.

He'd completely blanked on her name.

Something beginning with an *H*... Helen, Heidi.... *Crap.*

Ollie mentally listed all the *H* names he could think of, waiting for a pause in the conversation so he could apologise and ask the pretty blonde for her name again, but she continued talking as though her need to breathe was secondary to pushing words out of her mouth.

She was up from Adelaide... here for her cousin's wedding... yadda, yadda, yadda... and "Oh-em-gee, Melville's Crossing is just the cutest little town."

Oliver's eye twitched, and he forced a smile. "Melville's Cross," he said, cutting off her one-sided conversation.

"Pardon?"

"It's Melville's Cross, not Crossing."

The blonde shrugged and twirled a lock of long hair

around her slender fingers in a way designed to draw his attention back to her breasts. "What's the difference?"

"Well, 'crossing' would suggest John Melville was just passing through when he discovered the place," he said, making eye contact again, "and not looking to build a settlement."

The indifferent look on the woman's face told him there was little point in continuing the history lesson, so he smiled again and reached for his beer.

"So, what's there to do around here on a Friday night?"

Ten years ago—hell, twelve months ago—he would have suggested going back to wherever the lady was staying for a couple drinks and a night of no-holds-barred fucking. It was a routine he knew well, one that was beneficial to both parties involved and always ended amicably. Ollie got laid, the lady got an evening of pussy pampering, and everyone went home happy. Win-win.

But lately his thoughts on dating and relationships had taken a different turn, leaned towards something more real. More permanent.

Something more meaningful.

In the last year, his sister, Abby, and brothers Rafe and Toby had all found their perfect match.

After two unhealthy relationships, Abby had found someone who appreciated her, loved her for who she was and not what they wanted her to be.

And sixteen years of fighting their feelings came to a head when Rafe had *finally* married his soulmate—after he'd knocked her up and she'd almost married someone else, of course, but better late than never.

While Toby, the quiet giant Ollie had begun to assume would live forever as the world's most eligible bachelor, was getting married the following weekend to a woman who was not only a perfect match for his sexual proclivities but was just as much of a neat freak too.

He'd watched all of them enter their new—and, some would argue, improved—lives, and a part of him envied them for it. A part of himself he hadn't recognised in a very long time had started to make itself known again, craved what his siblings had found in the arms of another.

I should be so lucky.

But he also knew the woman sitting opposite him wasn't offering anything even remotely akin to a relationship.

As he watched her over the rim of his glass, Oliver knew this woman wasn't for him. Not long term. She was an out-of-towner attending a wedding and would be gone in forty-eight hours or less. Still, she was here now, and he could count on one finger the number of times he'd had sex in the last six months.

Permanent could wait a little longer.

He was about to suggest they get out of there when Dave, the publican, approached their table with the basket of hot chips Ollie had ordered before the pretty blonde caught his eye and he'd invited her to join him for a drink.

"Sorry to interrupt, Ollie," Dave said as he put the

food down, "but I was wondering if I could borrow a moment of your time." The older man glanced at... Haley? before landing back on him. *Shit.* He really needed to ask for her name again.

"Kinda in the middle of something here, Dave." He flashed an apologetic smile at his date. "Can it wait 'til another time?"

The old publican flicked his weary gaze between Oliver and his companion again, then shook his head and smiled tightly. "'Fraid not, son. It's a matter of some... delicacy."

Confusion warred with curiosity over his friend's meaning, which in turn warred with mild irritation at being interrupted. Ollie's balls were bluer than a clear summer sky, and his dick was already standing at half mast, eager to get better acquainted with... Heather?

But Oliver also knew Dave wouldn't have interrupted if whatever it was he wanted him for wasn't important.

Flashing another apologetic smile at his date, he said, "Sorry about this." Taking a twenty out of his wallet, he placed it on the table. "Why don't you refresh our drinks while I speak to my friend." Then he winked and grinned as she flashed him a coy smile of her own. "And help yourself to the chips before they go cold. I'll be back in a tick."

"A man willing to share his chips?" she said, her voice a smoky purr. "I'll definitely be waiting."

Slipping from the bar stool, Oliver followed Dave out through the kitchen to the rear of the pub. Plastic milk crates and wooden pallets were stacked against the back wall, and perched on top of one of those stacks was a hooded figure.

A woman, if he wasn't mistaken. Not that he could tell from the way she was dressed in baggy jeans and sneakers, nor by her face, which was obscured by the hoodie and the thick brown hair that had escaped it. He could hear the person muttering to themselves, but it was too quiet to make much sense of what was being said, let alone hear if the voice was feminine or not.

But all women moved in a certain way, and judging by her size and the way she jiggled her arse as she tried to get comfortable atop the stack of plastic crates, Ollie would bet good money he was right.

"Why am I here, Dave?" Ollie asked, watching the woman as she reached into her pocket and withdrew a small silver flask.

Dave gestured at their mystery guest. "Someone needs to take her home, and you're the only yahoo in there tonight," he said, thumbing over his shoulder at the pub, "who I trust to do just that." He sighed and rubbed at his grizzled jaw. "I'd take her if I could, but it's a Friday night, and I'm down two staff members. I'm swamped."

Ollie's confusion over the whole situation caused his brow to furrow tightly. What the hell did any of this have to do with him? But before he could ask, the woman cried out, "Oh shit!"

A second later, the stack of crates she was sitting on toppled over, sending her in a flailing heap towards the ground.

"Jesus." Both men rushed forwards, but Oliver was quicker. He caught her amid a hail of bouncing milk crates, preventing her from smacking face-first into the cold concrete. "I don't suppose you called Scott or Marie?" he said over his shoulder at Dave.

Surely helping a drunk woman was more in the realm of the local copper or his doctor girlfriend than a perverted blacksmith?

He helped the woman get back on her feet. "You all right, love?"

She kept her head down, hiding her face in the shadows of the hoodie, but nodded, so he let her go, holding his hands at the ready in case he had to catch her again. And thank goodness he had. Within seconds of letting go of her, her knees wobbled, seemingly unable to hold up her weight—slight as it was—and she crashed into him again. Her hands scrabbled in his shirtfront, popping a few buttons loose, and Ollie gritted his teeth to quell his irritation.

He had a sure thing waiting for him inside, but here he was, in the January heat and humidity with a drunk woman he didn't know clinging to him like a lifeboat. What the hell had he done to deserve this?

"For fuck's sake," he grumbled under his breath, then turned to Dave. "Call Scott and Marie. She needs help. Proper help."

In a display of strength he hadn't expected, the woman shoved out of his hold and began patting down her pockets. "Where is it?" she muttered quietly, and something about her voice pulled at him. Something old and remembered.

But before he could think too deeply on the matter, Dave growled at him.

"What the bloody hell do you think Scott or Marie can do for her that you can't? I just want to make sure she gets home safe and unmolested. And it's not like you have anything better to do."

Ollie's dick would disagree. "Did you not see the blonde I was sitting with?"

"Sure did." Dave lit up a cigarette, drew the smoke into his lungs, then raised one brow and exhaled through his nostrils, making him look like an annoyed dragon. "And I'll give you free chips and beer for a month if you can tell me her name."

Ollie narrowed his gaze and glared at the old man, then admitted defeat. "Shut up, Dave."

The publican grinned. "That's what I thought."

"It's not like she cares what my name is either, you know," he said, a resigned frown pulling at his mouth. "They never do."

The woman wandered away from the two men, her muttering voice teasing Ollie's senses again. It was so familiar, and yet... not. "I just had it. What did I do with it?" She kicked the milk crates out of her way.

"We can debate your dating practices another night. Right now I just—"

"Dave!" One of the cooks popped her head out the kitchen door. "We need you. It's getting crazy in here.

Oh, hey, Ollie," she added with a little wave, a bright smile lighting up her face when Oliver waved back.

One of the downsides to living in a small town: single men were at a premium, and everyone seemed to have a daughter or niece or cousin they wanted him to meet, even with his reputation as an unrelenting man-whore. But reputations aside, Ollie was also one of very few single blokes in town who had a steady income, and it never ceased to amaze him what people were willing to overlook when money was involved.

"I'll be there in a sec, Tammy," Dave said, stamping out his smoke, then waited for the girl to leave before continuing. "Listen, I know you've got a girl waiting for you inside, but you and I both know you'll be sitting on that same stool at the same time with a different blonde next Friday night."

He nodded towards the woman who'd wandered into the garden, still searching for whatever it was she thought she'd lost. "Here and now you have a friend in need, and I asked you to help her because you're a good man, Oliver. I know you two had a falling out, but I also know I can trust you to do the right thing and take care of her."

Ollie stared at Dave like the crazy person he obviously was. "What are you talking about?" he asked, then gestured to the woman. "I haven't got a clue who she is."

Dave's weathered face stretched into a look of disbelief, his bushy eyebrows shooting into his receding hairline. "You don't recognise her?"

Watching her as she walked back towards them, he

took in her unflattering outfit, the way her clothes hung off her—probably two sizes too big—and how she kept the hoodie pulled low over her eyes. She was taller than average, but so were a lot of women he knew. And while the brown hair escaping her hoodie had a distinct wave to it, that didn't help narrow it down either.

Her voice, however.... He knew that voice. Didn't he?

Caution tempered his words. "Should I recognise her?"

The publican sighed wearily as he moved to stand beside the woman and, against her drunken protests, yanked back the hoodie, revealing Ollie's former best friend.

The only person outside his family he'd do anything for.

"Mia."

2

T he blood drained from Oliver's face as a whirlwind of emotions gripped his spine and squeezed it like a vice. Shock, disbelief, anger, lust, longing, hurt....

There was a lot of hurt.

But all that took a back seat to the concern flooding through him at the sight of Major Emilia Caldwell in her current state.

Drunk.

Since when did Mia get drunk? But then he remembered he hadn't seen her in eighteen years, and all that anger and hurt came roaring back.

"Dave, I—"

"Gotta go, son," he said, slapping his shoulder. "I'm needed inside. But I trust you'll do the right thing, yeah?" And then the sneaky old bugger slipped back inside the pub, leaving Ollie to deal with Mia.

Mia, who was drunk.

"Fucking hell," he muttered, then dropped his head back and stared up at the night sky, silently praying for patience, because if there was one thing Oliver loathed, it was dealing with drunk people.

People with lowered inhibitions and a heightened sense of not giving a fuck. People who did and said things they would never remember while he was stuck with a head full of memories playing on an endless loop at the back of his mind in vivid fucking Technicolour.

"I never wanted you. I certainly never loved you. You were nothing more than a blip on my radar."

A loop he could never quite drown out, no matter how hard he tried.

He needed a distraction before the loop could snag on a particularly unpleasant thorn. And he'd never found anyone more distracting than Mia Caldwell.

Anchoring his hands on his hips, Oliver shifted his gaze to follow Mia as she continued poking around the edges of the garden beds. She looked so different from the girl he'd known. So worn around the edges. The baggy clothing didn't help, nor the way her hair hung limp around her face and neck, and maybe it was just the dim yellow glow cast by the light above the loading bay, but she looked much older than her thirty-five years.

This woman wasn't his Mia.

This woman was a stranger.

Oliver sighed quietly and shook his head. His Mia or not, she still needed help.

"What exactly do you think you've lost?"

She jumped at the sound of his voice, as though she'd forgotten he was there and was startled at the reminder she wasn't alone. She frowned. "My flask. I just had it."

Patience. "I think you've had enough for one night, don't you?"

That made her look at him. For the first time since he'd gone out there, she stopped hiding behind that bloody hoodie and finally looked directly at him.

Scowled at him was more appropriate. "I am not drunk!" Ollie raised one brow and continued staring at her until she lifted one shoulder in a half shrug. "Okay, fine. I'm a little bit tipsy," she conceded with a wave of her hand. "But I need my flask. I must've dropped it when I fell, so it has to be here somewhere."

"You don't need it, Mia."

She stilled for a moment, then continued searching. "It was Dad's," she said quietly.

Casting a quick glance around them, Oliver couldn't see the flask anywhere obvious, which meant it probably was in the garden somewhere, hidden within the lush tropical foliage. It wasn't going anywhere anytime soon. "We can come back tomorrow and look for it then."

"No. What if someone steals it?"

"This is Melville's Cross, sweetling. No one would dare steal your dad's flask."

"No one local," she grumbled. "I'm not worried about the locals."

She had a point. Unlike the Bennett family, the Caldwell family was well respected in their tiny town. No one would dare steal the late colonel's flask. But there were plenty of outsiders in town who wouldn't know the significance of the flask or what it meant to Mia, and while Ollie always sought out the best in people and hoped whoever found it would turn it in, he was all too aware of the worst in people too. He knew it was possible some wanker would find the family keepsake and pocket it without a second thought.

"How about this? I'll come back and find it after I take you home, okay?"

Mia stared up at him, her eyes glistening in the dull light. "Really?"

Was it really so surprising that someone would do something nice for her? Or was it just because it was him making the offer? Either way, he nodded. "Really, really."

A small smile preceded an even smaller exhalation of breath, one of relief, if he had to guess. "Thanks, Ollie. You're a good friend."

Restraining the urge to snort, Oliver helped Mia over to the milk crates again, flipped one over, and eased her down onto it. "I have to say goodnight to someone, and then we'll go. Will you be okay for a minute?"

"I'm not an invalid," she snapped, suddenly scowling again. "I'll be fine."

Ollie arched one brow at the vehemence of her statement. "Okay." Then with one last glance to make sure she actually was fine, he said, "I'll be back soon."

Slipping through the kitchen and back inside the

pub, he sought out... *fuck*. Whatever her name was. Not that it mattered now.

Wending his way through the much larger crowd, Oliver found the blonde sitting at the same table with an empty chip basket and two other local blokes ogling her tits. Ordinarily he would have used his superior height and size to his advantage and scared them away, reclaimed his seat at the table, but considering his current situation with Mia, who was he to spoil anyone's fun? Especially since he wouldn't be partaking of it himself. And it wasn't as if the lady in question seemed to mind the attention, judging by the way she leaned closer to Tom and Baz, flashing them one of those coy little smiles she'd used on him earlier.

"I'm sorry," he said, approaching the table. "That took longer than expected."

The blonde whipped her head around to stare at him, her eyes wide and her mouth open. The local boys glared at him, probably expecting him to steal away their prize. Hell, it wasn't Ollie's fault he'd been blessed with his father's natural charisma and his mother's Nordic good looks. He couldn't help it if women naturally gravitated towards him. Not that he usually did much to dissuade them either.

Tonight's your lucky night, boys.

"You've been gone so long I honestly didn't think you were coming back," Blondie stammered, flicking a nervous glance at her new companions and then at the chip basket. "I ate all your chips."

Oliver chuckled. "A fair price to pay for my rudeness. Especially since I can't stay."

"What?" all three of them said at once. Blondie sounded like she wasn't sure if she was disappointed or not, while Tom and Baz sounded perfectly happy about the sudden turn of events.

"A friend of mine isn't feeling well. I need to make sure she gets home okay."

"Aww, what a sweet gesture," Tom said, making zero attempt to hide his sarcasm.

"Yeah, you take care now, Bennett," Baz added, slapping his hand on Ollie's shoulder and giving him a shove. At least he tried to, but standing at five feet and nine inches to Ollie's six feet and five, and working at a desk all day compared to pounding hot metal on an anvil, Baz had as much of a chance at shoving Ollie away as a chihuahua did to a Great Dane.

Ignoring the guys, Ollie held out his hand to Blondie and smiled. "It was very nice meeting you. Have fun at your cousin's wedding. And if you're ever this far north again, I hope you'll stop by and say g'day."

He turned to leave, but she grabbed his wrist. "That's it? Just... see ya later? You invited me for a drink and now you're blowing me off for another woman?"

"For a friend who needs my help, yes," he said more calmly than he felt, suddenly feeling a lot less guilty about forgetting her name. "And excuse me for saying so," he added drily, "but it didn't really look like you were missing me. So goodnight. And fellas"—he shot Tom and

Baz a look that communicated exactly how glad he was to be leaving—"good luck."

The guys hid their chuckles behind their pint glasses while Blondie huffed, looking miffed that anyone would dare to dismiss her so readily.

Oliver made a beeline for the back door of the pub and the cranky wench he hoped was still waiting for him.

3

Mia awoke with a jolt and blindly swung her fist, flinching when she connected with something fleshy.

"What the hell, Mia? It's me. It's Ollie."

Pushing back her hoodie just far enough to see the big man crouching in front of her, she winced when she saw him cupping his cheek. "Sorry, force of habit," she grumbled.

His eyes widened momentarily as he absorbed her unintentional admission, then softened with sympathy, with *pity*. Like she needed any of that.

Clenching her jaw, she looked away.

"No, I'm sorry, sweetling," Oliver said gently. "I should have made some noise before approaching you. I didn't realise you'd fallen asleep."

His rich voice smoothed her ruffled feathers, something she found to be both a comfort and a nuisance. She hadn't seen the man since they were seventeen. How the hell did he still have such an effect on her? He didn't even sound the same as he had back then, and except for his height and the colour of his hair, he didn't much look the same either.

Instead of the lean, clean running machine she'd crushed on as a girl, the man before her was a bearded brute, his long dark-blond hair pulled up in a ridiculous yet artfully messy man-bun, and a tattoo of runes wrapped around one thick forearm.

His eyes were different too. Not their colour, they were still the same beautiful blue they'd always been, but a world-weary shadow marred their depths. Dulled their once brilliant shine.

Not that she could talk.

She'd changed so much her childhood friend hadn't recognised her at all.

It wasn't as if she'd been trying to hide her identity from him. Well, maybe she had, a little bit. But it was more embarrassment than anything that had kept her tugging her hoodie down to hide her eyes. Not because she'd been drinking, because honestly, she was nowhere near as drunk as Ollie and Dave seemed to think. Certainly not enough to cause such a fuss.

In truth, she was tired.

And in pain.

It was purely bad timing that had seen her stumble and fall in front of Dave. *Nosy old publican.* At least he wasn't a gossip.

He'd been sitting in the loading bay, smoking a durry,

when she'd emerged from the goat track that cut through the gardens at the rear of the pub.

It was her first night back in her tiny hometown, and after dumping her car at the house, she'd gone to the cemetery to visit her parents' graves. She hadn't even bothered to change out of her travelling clothes first.

Mia had sat with her parents for hours, talking and sipping scotch, telling them everything and anything about the past two years, all in a vain attempt to avoid going home to an empty house filled with rotting furniture and mixed emotional memories.

Only when the daylight had faded enough for the street lamps to flicker on did she notice how late it was and concede to her fate: a lonely night in an echoey house where the wind whistled through the cracks in the windows and the floorboards creaked with age.

The decision to cut through the pub gardens had been one of pure economy. A time saver to get her off her feet faster and ease the ache in her back and hip. But Dave had spotted her and called out her name, and instead of watching where she was putting her feet, Mia had stumbled and fallen.

When he'd helped her up again, he'd smelled the alcohol on her breath, assumed the worst, propped her up against the milk crates, and gone to fetch her some help.

She'd almost wished she *were* drunk when he came back with Oliver Bennett in tow. At least then there would have been a chance she'd forget any of this ever happened. But that wasn't to be, because as she sat there listening to the pair of them arguing about Ollie's sex life, her lower back had spasmed, and when she'd moved to ease the pain, she'd lost her balance. And then she'd lost her father's flask.

The one he'd given her after her graduation from Duntroon.

The one his father had given him at his graduation.

"So, what now?" she asked, pushing to her feet, making Oliver back up and out of her space.

Her embarrassment was making her snippy, and why wouldn't it? She'd almost ripped his shirt open, for fuck's sake, and she'd have to have been blind to miss the hint of chiselled pecs decorated with dark blond hair that had appeared in the V she'd created when his buttons had popped open. *Stupid hip.* Buttons he'd since refastened, hiding that tantalising slice of tanned perfection.

"You going to hold my hand and look both ways before letting me cross the street?"

Oliver closed his eyes and breathed slowly, like he was trying very hard not to snap at her. Her embarrassment momentarily forgotten, Mia almost laughed. Usually she was the one closing her eyes and counting to ten so she didn't throttle someone.

"No," he said, staring down at her once more. "I'm going to do as Dave asked and walk you home, and then I'm going to bed. Alone. Again." His eyes narrowed slightly. "Can you walk?"

Biting her tongue to stop herself from snapping at him and his assumptions again, she deliberately batted her eyelashes and threw down some sarcasm instead. "If I say no, will you give me a piggyback ride?"

Her irritation was short-lived. For the first time since seeing him tonight, his lips twitched up in a sexy half-smile, and little crinkles appeared around his eyes, softening his stern appearance and making her heartbeat quicken. "If I give you a piggyback ride, do you promise not to throw up on me again?"

She jabbed a finger into his chest. "That only happened once, and it was your own bloody fault for bouncing me up and down. I told you I didn't feel well."

"And I told you not to eat all those hot dogs."

"Your brother bet me I couldn't do it."

"Charlie bets people can't do stupid shit all the time," he said, that sexy half-smile now a full-blown grin. "Doesn't mean you should do it."

Mia fully intended to continue arguing her point, even planted her hands on her hips for emphasis, but after opening her mouth, she promptly shut it again. Not because she had nothing to say but because her words had dissolved into laughter, and she was trying valiantly to keep it jammed in her throat where it belonged.

She was mad at him, damn it. The last thing she needed was to lose ground by laughing.

But then, like the proverbial light bulb flickering above her head, Mia realised something.

As of forty-eight hours earlier, she was no longer a soldier. She didn't have to win on principle. She didn't have to stand her ground, even when she was dog tired and in more pain than one human being should ever have to be.

She didn't have to suck it up and shove it down and pretend she wasn't furious just so no one could accuse her of being overly emotional, or crack jokes about "parting the Red Sea", or try to cop a feel and suggest all she needed was a good fuck.

Nor was she staring down an insubordinate shithead who couldn't wrap his pea-sized intellect around the fact that a woman was in charge, that she held all the power.

This was Oliver Bennett. One of Ulysses Bennett's infamous bastard sons. To say he'd been raised in a sex-positive environment was an understatement. And not just about having sex but in attitudes towards the opposite sex.

This was Ollie she was talking to, and Mia had nothing to prove, so she took a breath and let her laughter out.

Once that seal was broken and her laughter bubbled free, she found she couldn't stop... until her hip decided it was a good time to act out and she found herself twisting her fingers in Ollie's shirtfront again, trying desperately to breathe through the pain.

Big, warm hands gripped her forearms, and panic stained his deep voice. "Mia, what's wrong?"

"I'm okay," she lied. "It's just my hip. Well, my back and my hip. Well, my back, my hip, and my knee." She tilted her forehead against Oliver's chest and breathed deeply, sucking his deliciously masculine scent into her lungs. "I just need a minute for the muscle spasms to pass."

He swore quietly. "You didn't fall down because you were drinking, did you?"

She shook her head. "No, I—" Another violent spasm cut her words short. She rolled her lips between her teeth to silence her cries, but nothing could stop the tears from leaking down her cheeks and dripping onto Ollie's shirt.

His grip tightened on her arms. "Tell me what to do. Tell me what you need."

Taking another deep breath, Mia lifted her head and stared at his chest. A few more breaths and she could ignore enough of the pain that she lifted her gaze to his.

Swallowing hard, she said, "I need to walk it off, and then I need a heat pack." Seeing the panic in Ollie's eyes forced her to grin and make light of the situation. No sense in both of them suffering. "And painkillers. A big fistful of painkillers." But eighteen years apart had done nothing to quash Oliver's ability to see right through her, and admittedly, her attempt at humour had fallen flat even to her ears.

Scowling, Oliver hooked his arm around Mia's back and tucked his hand under her arm, then pulled her close to his side and started moving them in the direction of her house.

"Lean on me," he said, his familiar scent and gentle touch doing more to ease her anguish than her therapist ever could.

"Thanks, Ollie," she said quietly. "I appreciate this."

A grunt was his only reply, which made her smile—a genuine smile—despite her discomfort. "And, Ollie?"

"Hmm?"

"I missed you."

For the briefest of moments, his arm tightened around her. "I missed you too, sweetling."

Sweetling. The endearment made her heartbeat quicken, but it wouldn't stop her from telling him a hard truth. "And, Ollie?"

He shifted her against his side as he helped her step over the curb. "Yes?"

Mia reached up and cupped his cheek, made him look at her. "I hate your hair."

4

Ten minutes—and one contentious discussion about man-buns—later, they approached Mia's childhood home. Walking unaided was no longer an issue, but her back and hip still ached from the severity of the muscle spasms. At least she could walk again without fear of falling flat on her face.

That was until they reached the front steps.

Her family home was an old Queenslander, a large weatherboard box set on stumps and surrounded on all sides by a deep timber veranda. As Mia stared at the ten steps leading up to the latticework gate and the front door beyond that, her shoulders slumped and her stomach filled with acid. The railing had long since rotted away, leaving her with nothing to lean on as she climbed to the top.

If she'd been on her own, she would have crawled up the stairs on her hands and knees or sat on her arse and gone up them backwards. But with Oliver standing beside her, watching her with his careful gaze, she'd rather face the lesser of two evils and beg for more of his help than humiliate herself further by crawling.

Gritting her teeth, she said, "Can you—" She cut herself off and shook her head, angry that something so simple felt so utterly insurmountable.

"What do you need?" he asked, his words spoken so gently it brought tears to her eyes.

Mia was—had been—a major in the Royal Australian Army. She'd held company records for running, swimming, and shooting. She'd commanded troops in a war zone, for fuck's sake. She would not be defeated by a flight of fucking stairs.

One hand balled into a fist at her side, the other fell to grip her leg just below her hip. "I... I can't lift my leg high enough to walk up the stairs unaided." She'd whispered the words, but in the still of the summer night, she may as well have yelled them. "If the railing was still here, I—"

"Say it."

Her brow pinched. "Say what?"

"You know what," he said, smirking. "Say it."

Helplessness replaced by frustration, Mia let loose an irritated sigh. "Seriously?"

Ollie cupped his hand behind one ear. "Whenever you're ready."

"*Ugh*. Fine. I'm sorry I said your man-bun looks stupid, okay?"

"And?"

"Really?" She growled and glared up at his smirking

face. The bastard cocked one brow and folded his arms across his chest. Oliver Bennett was just as stubborn as she was, worse sometimes. "Fine," she said again, huffing and rolling her eyes. "And your beard doesn't makes you look like a hipster."

His smirk broadened into a full-blown grin. "That wasn't so hard now, was it?"

Before she knew what he was doing, Oliver had scooped her up, and she had to wrap her arms around his neck or risk falling to the ground. A few seconds later, his long legs had carried her to the top of the stairs and through the gate, delivering her to the front door.

"Keys?" he asked as he put her down again, holding out his hand expectantly.

Mia fished her keys out of her back pocket, but she didn't hand them over. "I'm more than capable of opening the front door without your help," she said, inserting the key into the lock. But when she went to turn it, it wouldn't budge.

"You sure about that?"

She pulled the key out, stuck it in again, and gave it a good jiggle, but to no avail. "What the bloody hell is wrong with this thing?"

Ollie stuck out his hand again. "Keys," he said, and this time it wasn't a request.

Frowning, Mia handed them over.

"If you'd bothered to visit Rafe when you got back to town like you were supposed to, he would have given you a new set of keys," he said, threading a link with three new keys on it onto her keychain.

"I can understand why Rafe has keys to my mother's house," she said, one brow winging up in question, "but why do you?"

"As your mother's lawyer, Rafe had the locks changed last year. There was an... incident last August. Someone was discovered squatting in another vacant house." He held out what she assumed was the new front door key. Taking it, she inserted it into the lock. "And I have a set because I do maintenance around the place when I can. Which, I'm sorry to say, hasn't been as often as I'd like since Louisa passed."

Mia was about to pop open the door when a wave of sadness crashed over her. She'd only been half listening to Ollie as she'd turned the new key and felt the lock disengage, but now that she was about to enter the house, the house her parents had named Someday, she felt something tighten around her heart, threatening to crush it.

Her mother, Louisa Caldwell, beloved high school music teacher, had died two years earlier, and her death had ripped through Mia like a bullet through glass, shattering her into a million tiny pieces. Her mother had been her rock, her best friend, and confidant. Her biggest cheerleader and her most constructive critic. She'd always been so energetic, seemed so indestructible, even though she'd been dying.

"Cancer's no excuse not to get shit done," she'd say before mowing the yard, or painting the kitchen, or interfering in Mia's haphazard love life.

Another wave of grief rolled over her, and the

squeezing around her heart intensified. "I can't do this," she said, dropping her hand from the door handle. Her nose prickled, and tears glazed her eyes. "I'm not ready."

As her tears began streaming down her cheeks, Ollie pulled Mia into his arms and held on tight, letting her sob and wail until she had nothing left. Until she sagged against him, exhausted and wrung out.

Oliver locked the door and pocketed the keys. "Come on, sweetling," he said, gently steering her back down the steps. "You can stay at The Forge." When he reached the bottom, he turned away, bent forwards slightly, and looked back over his shoulder. "You still want that piggy-back ride?"

Mia was so stunned by the unexpected offer that it forced a laugh to escape her and chased away a little of her grief.

Very little, but enough.

She sniffed and swiped at the tears that refused to stop rolling down her face, then smiled at her friend and nodded, as though not a day had passed since she'd seen him last.

As if it were possible to simply pick up where they'd left off so long ago.

"Yes, please. I'd like that very much."

"Then climb on," Ollie said, winking. "And let's go home."

5

Mia opened her eyes and immediately shut them again, growling ineffectually at the bright sunlight flooding the room. But a deep chuckling sound made her peek them open again.

"Good morning," Oliver said, grinning from his spot at the door, leaning against the frame with his arms folded over his broad chest and his bare feet crossed at the ankles.

What was it about men—this man in particular—that looked so fucking good in blue jeans and a T-shirt? Was it the way the denim taunted her, clinging lovingly to his firm arse and strong thighs? Or maybe how the soft cotton of his shirt stretched thin over his arms and torso, showing off muscles he definitely didn't have the last time she saw him?

Was it wrong to be jealous of a T-shirt?

But then she didn't look the same as she did at seventeen either.

Not by a long shot.

She'd always been slim, but years of daily training had added lean muscle to her slender frame. And the hair she'd always worn as long as possible in school was now trimmed to a more sensible shoulder-length.

"Morning," Mia said, sitting up, rubbing the sleep from her eyes to hide the fact she'd been ogling Ollie. "Did you open the curtains?"

"Guilty," he said, entirely too cheerfully for Mia's liking.

A morning person she was not.

"What time is it?" she grumbled.

"Around nine. I thought you might like a sleep-in now that you're old and retired."

Mia flipped him off, then tossed back the covers and gingerly shifted her feet to the floor, testing her leg before putting any weight on it. "I didn't retire, you arse. I was medically discharged. Big difference."

When he didn't respond, she glanced back over at him and saw him staring at her. More accurately, he was staring at her legs—her very long, very *naked* legs—and working his way up from there. And it wasn't as if she was actually naked, she was wearing the same thing she always wore to bed: cotton undies and a tank top.

It wasn't her fault the clothing hugged her lithe figure like a second skin, and she could have been mistaken, but was that Ollie's tongue flicking out to moisten his lips?

A little shiver of excitement skittered over her flesh, and she wasn't ashamed to admit she liked him looking at her. She'd always liked Oliver Bennett looking at her, and she had first-hand experience of all the things he could do with that tongue.

Resisting the urge to press her thighs together and give herself—and her increasingly wet pussy—away, she said, "Can I help you with something?"

Quickly shifting his gaze elsewhere, Ollie cleared his throat and pointed to her ech-bag on the floor at the foot of the bed. And the walking stick her therapist had insisted she start using to aid her mobility. The one Mia had stubbornly left in the car with the rest of her stuff when she'd visited her parents' graves.

"I, uh, drove your car over and brought your gear inside. Is that really all you brought with you?"

Mia shrugged. "Eighteen years of living on army bases," she said, trying to make it sound less pathetic than it actually was. "I don't own a lot of stuff so I tend to travel light."

Oliver grinned again and scrubbed one hand across the nape of his neck. "Yeah, I get it. Until recently, the only stuff I owned were some tools, a pair of boots, three pairs of jeans, and about fifty T-shirts. And well, my, uh...." He cleared his throat and pushed away from the door frame. "Never mind. I'll let you get dressed. Do you need anything?"

The sudden change of topic made Mia grin. As did his T-shirt, which she'd only just noticed had the words "Blacksmiths Like It Hot And Heavy" printed across his muscled chest. It was a distracting sight, to be sure, but not as interesting as Ollie's embarrassment.

"Hang on. Back up," she said. "Finish what you were going to say. A pair of boots, three pairs of jeans, fifty T-shirts, and...." She stared at him expectantly.

He dropped his chin to his chest and sighed heavily. "My re-enactment gear." After a moment he lifted his gaze, his deep blue eyes narrowed slightly as they bored into hers, like he was expecting her to ridicule him. "My Viking kit. Clothes, boots, weapons, shields—"

The thought of tall, sexy Oliver dressed as a Viking had Mia far too curious to make fun of him. What she really wanted to ask him was if he wore leather pants like they did in the movies and on tele but decided to stick with something safer. Something more like neutral ground.

"Do you have one of those big tents with the cross-beams?" She crossed her arms at the wrists to demonstrate her meaning.

One corner of Oliver's mouth hitched up in a half-grin and he nodded. "Yes."

"Are the beams carved or plain? And do you have the whole demountable bed set-up, or do you sleep in a swag on the ground?"

Now his grin stretched all the way across his face and both eyebrows slid up as he stared at her, his question silent yet obvious.

"What? You honestly think I would have survived almost two whole decades in the army if I didn't like camping?"

"Oh *riiight*, you're asking me about the bed I sleep in because you 'like camping'. Uh-huh."

Heat prickled over Mia's body in all the right places as Ollie turned the topic around on her and made it decidedly *not* neutral ground.

What the fuck was she thinking?

Oh, yeah, she wasn't. Because the walking embodiment of all her wet dreams rolled into one still held the power to suck her brain dry of all common sense.

Before her useless brain could form a response, Oliver said, "Maybe you should join me sometime."

Wait. What? Did he just invite her to fuck him...? "Join you?" she asked, cautiously.

"At the next re-enactment," he clarified with a knowing smirk. Bastard knew exactly where her mind had gone.

Straight into the gutter.

Where all dirty, dirty things belonged.

Now she fought off a different kind of heat. That of embarrassment. She scoffed. Like she'd ever let that beat her. Mia lifted one brow. "Do I have to dress up like a Viking?"

"Hmm,"—he scrubbed his hand across his short beard while he pretended to think—"do you have to dress up like a kick-arse warrior woman and go to battle for the honour and glory of your family?" Then he dropped all pretence and looked directly at her, hitting her with the full force of his baby-blues and that sexy grin. "Yes. Yes you do."

Mia burst out laughing. "You're such a dork," she said, her laugh softening into a smile. "I'm glad some things haven't changed."

"Hey, I think you'd make a great shield maiden. It's basically the same job you've been doing for the last eighteen years but in cooler clothes and with a sword."

"Oh shut up," she chuckled, then winced and hissed out a breath as she got to her feet. The ache in her back was still there, and she needed a good stretch to sort out her leg, but it didn't hurt too badly, all things considered.

In the blink of an eye, Ollie was by her side, all humour gone from his expression. "Do you need help?" he asked, his voice almost a full octave higher than it had been a minute ago and edged with panic.

She shook her head and waved him off. "I'm all right. It's my own fault. I shouldn't have driven straight through from Sydney to home yesterday. Fourteen hours in the driver's seat put too much pressure on my back. I'll run through my Pilates routine after breakfast, stretch out this leg and work on my core." She flashed him a slightly pained smile. "You're welcome to join me."

Oliver stepped back and gave her space. "Pilates?" His laugh was almost as pained as hers. "Ah... no. I don't think so. Anyway, I only came in here to tell you breakfast is ready. So why don't you get dressed, and we'll meet you in the kitchen."

"We?"

"Yeah, Rafe and Jane got here about half an hour ago, and Abby and Wolf just pulled up out front. They flew back from Sydney first thing this morning." He winked, and it made her stomach flutter. "See you out there," he said, then shut the door, giving her some privacy.

"I guess the gang's all here," Mia muttered as she stretched her arms over her head and yawned loudly.

Out of all of Oliver's siblings, Abby and Rafe were the two she'd most associated with over the years, although she hadn't seen either of them since her mother's funeral.

It had always felt a bit weird, talking to the pair of them when she hadn't spoken to Oliver for so long, but she had a hunch they knew the reasons behind that decision. They were just too polite to point them out.

They also hadn't pointed out how dumb those reasons truly were, for which she'd be forever grateful.

She'd come to realise exactly how much of an idiot she'd been as time wore on, but the longer things went unsaid, the harder it was to say them.

No matter how much she may have wanted to.

Eventually she'd learned to let those things go and put the whole situation down to the stupidity of youth. After all, what could be more stupid than falling in love with your best friend, seducing him and then running away from the messy emotional fallout of that decision?

She sighed heavily.

No one ever said love was logical.

Pulling on a pair of yoga pants and a fitted T-shirt—and continuing to ignore the bloody walking stick—Mia went through her usual morning routine, then made her way out to the kitchen. The room was filled with happy people and the smell of a home-cooked breakfast.

The scene couldn't be any more different from that of an officers' mess on any given morning, a spectacle of arrogant self-righteousness, dipped in entitlement and reeking of toxic masculinity and imported cigars.

The culture shock almost brought her to her knees. *Maybe I should have grabbed the stupid stick.*

"That smells amazing," she said, stepping into the room.

"Mia!" Jane Melville and Abby Bennett cried out at once, their happy faces and open arms making her feel more welcome than she deserved. Within seconds she was being squished between the two women, surrounded by their enthusiasm and one very pregnant belly.

She repressed a pained groan as they put pressure on her leg and painted on her everything-is-fine face.

"Whoa! Did someone just kick me?" she said, easing back from Jane, staring down at the smaller woman with awe. "How far along are you? You look ready to burst."

"Oh my God, I was ready to burst around Christmas, but the little buggers aren't due until February. And yeah, sorry, they're kicking a lot this morning. When I get excited, they get excited, and then it's just one big free-for-all."

Mia quickly hid a smile behind her hand. Jane had always possessed the power to talk faster than a speeding train and it seemed nothing had changed.

The gold band on her wedding finger was new though, as was the matching ring on Rafe's hand. She was certain he hadn't been wearing it when she saw him two years earlier, so maybe this was a recent development?

When Rafe stepped forwards and draped his arms around Jane, clasped her hands in his, and rested them on her enormous belly, Mia had her answer.

"Breathe, beautiful," Rafe told the bouncy redhead, a light chuckle and an indulgent smile accompanying his words.

So protective.

So loving.

Mia's inner romantic sighed at the adorable couple. "So, you two are married now?"

"Yep," Jane said, beaming at her as she tugged Rafe's arms tighter around her middle. "I'm Jane Melville-Bennett now. Rafe made a respectable woman of me in November."

"Respectable?" Her husband laughed. "I hope not."

"And did you say 'they' earlier?" Mia asked, pointing at Jane's belly. "As in more than one?"

Jane grinned. "Yep. Twin girls. We haven't decided on names yet, but—"

"Enough gasbagging." Oliver made an exasperated sound from the far end of the kitchen. "Food's getting cold, and I'm starving." He nodded at Mia. "Take a seat, sweetling. I'll bring you a plate."

Mia scowled at Ollie. Eighteen years apart had apparently done nothing to curb his bossiness. "Like I told you last night, I'm not an invalid. I can get my own food."

Ollie scowled back at her and his voice dipped lower, making her insides quiver with awareness and her fists clench in denial. "That was never in doubt. But you *are* my guest, so sit your arse down and let me take care of you."

Opening her mouth to spit out her reply, Mia never got the chance, because the man who'd been hovering by Abby's side and watching the exchange between the two of them with undisguised glee stuck out his hand. "I'm Wolf, by the way. Wolf Adams. Abby's fiancé."

Clamping her mouth shut, Mia shifted her narrowed gaze from Ollie to Wolf, shook his proffered hand, and took the seat next to him. "Mia Caldwell. Good to meet you."

"Likewise. I've been wanting to meet the infamous Major Mia for a while now."

Mia laughed, a burst of sound that eased her tension. "Infamous?"

"Yes, I was told something about you putting a boy in his place when he harassed you at school? As an ex-high school teacher," Wolf said, a cheeky glint in his eyes, "I'd be very interested to hear what happened."

A plate piled high with French toast, bacon, eggs over easy, sausages, and hash browns appeared in front of her, banging on the scrubbed wooden surface of the table as though it had been put there with force.

Flicking her gaze to Oliver's, Mia found he was glaring at his sister instead, undoubtedly for sharing information he'd rather keep quiet. She wasn't surprised. Ollie hated the story Wolf was referring to, but not for the reasons people suspected.

"Mia didn't just put him in his place," Abby said

around a mouthful of French toast. "She put him in an ambulance."

"And she was almost expelled because of it," Oliver snapped before taking the seat opposite Mia and attacking his breakfast like it was the enemy. His knife and fork scraped against the plate with such force she was amazed it didn't crack in two.

Rafe, ever the diplomat of the family, said, "Maybe you could discuss it another time. After Mia's had a chance to settle back in to small-town life. Assuming, of course, that you're sticking around for a while?"

Mia would've had to be deaf, dumb, and blind not to notice Oliver's big body go suddenly very still.

"I'd always intended to return home sooner or later," she said, keeping her voice carefully neutral. "I guess now that I'm old and retired, it turned out to be sooner."

Oliver didn't look at her, but his shoulders relaxed, and his food demolition became a lot less violent.

An awkward silence fell over the room, and for a short time, the only sounds were that of people chewing. The noise made Mia feel like someone was driving a nail through her eye, so she was relieved when Abby spoke up.

"Who wants a cuppa?"

"Coffee for me, *liebchen*," Wolf said, smacking Abby's arse as she rose from her seat, making her blush.

"Me too." Rafe.

"And me." Jane.

"She'll have tea," Rafe said, scowling at his wife.

Jane smiled sweetly back. "You do remember our deal, don't you, dearest?"

Rafe snorted. "I'm pretty sure my balls are safe."

"You have to sleep sometime," Jane said, winking.

But her husband didn't budge. "Tea or decaf, beautiful. Pick one."

"Fine," she conceded with a huff. "Tea, please."

Abby shook her head at her siblings, then looked at her. "Something for you, Mia?"

"I'll have tea, thanks."

"Black with honey and lemon," Oliver added as he finished his breakfast.

Mia stared at him in surprise. "You remember how I take my tea?"

Oliver looked at her then, a small smile on his face and a softness in his eyes that made her swallow thickly against the knot of emotion clogging her throat. "I'm glad you're home," he said quietly, ignoring her question, then pushed his chair away from the table and stood. "I have to get to work. Come find me when you're done, yeah?"

Mia nodded. "Will do."

Then Ollie dumped his plate in the sink and left the kitchen.

Just as she was finishing her tea, she heard the rhythmic *clang, clang, clang* of metal on metal and smiled to herself. It was a sound she knew well, one she'd grown up listening to and one she hadn't realised she'd missed until that moment.

Her emotions swelled inside her. She'd missed a lot

of things over the years. Looking around the table, listening to the easy flow of conversation and laughter, she realised she'd missed a lot of people too. Friends she'd abandoned when she'd run away from home and joined the circus commonly known as the Royal Australian Army.

But instead of crying about it, she did what she'd been trained to do and shoved the feelings down deep, locking them back in their cage until she was ready to deal with them.

Which was never.

Getting to her feet, Mia gathered her dishes and placed them beside the sink, but when she made to help with the washing up, Rafe and Abby shooed her out of the kitchen. "You're our guest," Abby said, then pulled her in for another hug. "We're all really glad you're home, Mia."

"Thanks, Abbs," Mia said, and hugged the woman back a little tighter. "I should go do my Pilates."

"On the back deck is the best place to do that," Jane said as she waddled closer, one hand pressed into the small of her back. "The guys rebuilt it before Christmas, made it bigger. There's lots of room to move now."

"Out the back, huh?" Right where Ollie would be working. "Thanks for the tip."

6

Oliver trained his focus on the red-hot iron in his hands as he moulded it into shape. Nothing could silence his mind quite like work did.

The rhythm of the strikes, the heat of the forge, the sweat running down his back. It wasn't just the routine of it but the simple joy of creating each object, of knowing each thing he made had purpose.

But nothing would silence his thoughts today.

Nothing would calm his mind while Emilia Caldwell lived under his roof, wearing those skimpy little panties and tit-hugging tank-tops.

Certainly not while she was planking in the backyard wearing skin-tight work-out gear, her firm arse pointed squarely in his direction.

Not that he was sad to see the departure of those baggy jeans and hoodie; her travelling clothes if he had to guess, given what she'd told him before breakfast.

He let his gaze travel the full length of her fit body.

Jesus, how the fuck does she hold that pose for so long?

His abs hurt just thinking about it.

His cock twitched at the same thought.

Watching her move into the next stretch, he saw her eyes pinch shut and her teeth sink into her bottom lip. Then he heard her cry out and clutch her thigh, and the next thing he knew he was kneeling beside her, easing her onto the deck.

"What do you need?"

"Heat," she said through gritted teeth. "I need to apply heat."

"On it."

Ripping his leather apron off as he ran to the kitchen, Ollie ransacked the drawers, looking for the heat pack he'd given Mia the night before.

He was sure he'd left it on the table, but where the fuck was it now?

"What the hell are you doing?" Abby said, putting away the clean dishes as she stared at him like he'd lost his mind.

"Mia needs a heat pack. Now!"

"It's in the pantry on the top shelf."

Finding the wheat-filled pillow exactly where his sister said it would be, Ollie shoved it in the microwave, then tapped his foot as he watched the clock counting down.

Who knew two minutes could last so fucking long?

When the timer dinged, he wrenched open the microwave, grabbed the pack, and ran back to Mia's side.

The blood drained from his face.

She was writhing on the deck, clutching her leg and biting her lip so hard it had darkened to a deep red.

"Got the pack. Tell me what to do," he said, dropping to her side.

Mia snatched the heat pack out of Ollie's hands and pressed it against her inner thigh. Her teeth released her lip, and she let out a shuddering breath. A few more seconds passed before her body relaxed enough that her eyes refocused on him before darting away again.

"Thank you," she murmured, a deep blush staining her neck and cheeks.

"You're welcome," he said, rubbing his neck to ease his own sudden awkwardness. Then he remembered his manners and offered to help her up.

"Thank you. Again," Mia said as Ollie eased her down onto the old daybed that sat pressed against the back wall of the house, overlooking the garden and forge. She continued pressing the heat pack to her thigh.

After a while, her breathing returned to normal and she didn't appear to be in pain anymore, but the tightening of her mouth every now and then told him she still was. She'd just gotten better at hiding it.

Ollie opened his mouth to ask her what happened, but when she averted her gaze again, he understood. At least he thought he did.

Mia hated showing weakness.

She always had, even in front of him. So whenever he knew she was hurting, either physically or emotionally, he'd always pretended he hadn't noticed and distracted her with a joke or idle chatter.

But not this time.

This time he wanted answers. He wanted to know what was going on with her, physically and emotionally. Because that was what grown-ups did.

They didn't hide from their problems, they sucked it up and faced them head-on.

And being there for each other during the whole "not hiding from, sucking it up, and facing problems head-on" thing was what best friends did.

"What's going on with you, with your leg?"

Mia scowled and avoided his gaze. "It's nothing. A leg cramp, that's all."

"Bullshit. You used to get leg cramps all the time after track-and-field training, and they never looked anything like that. So what's really going on? Does it have something to do with why you were discharged?"

Shifting in her seat and adjusting the heat pack again, Mia sat in silence and continued scowling at nothing in particular, so Oliver took a breath and tried a different tactic.

"Hey," he said, gently bumping his shoulder against hers. "This is me you're talking to. You always used to tell me everything."

She snorted and shook her head. "That was a long time ago, Bennett."

Ollie cocked one brow. "Bennett? Really? I'm not one of your little toy soldiers, Mia."

"Of course not," she said, looking mildly offended.

"My diggers were better behaved and knew not to question me."

"Noted," Ollie replied, grinning. "But if you call me Bennett again, I will tickle you until you get the hiccoughs. Because I know how much you *love* getting the hiccoughs."

Mia hated getting the hiccoughs.

Once, when they were fifteen, she'd gotten them so bad she'd actually thrown up. She'd then continued with a weird combination of hiccoughing and vomit-scented belching for another hour after that. To date, it was the most disgusting thing Oliver had ever seen. Even worse than the hot dog incident.

But at least his threat made her look at him. Glare at him, actually, but it was better than her avoiding him.

"Fine," she said through gritted teeth. "You really want to know what's going on with me?"

"I wouldn't have asked if I didn't."

She stuck out her chin and forced a tight-lipped smile that made his balls shrink. "I have arthritis."

Pretty sure he'd heard her wrong, Ollie frowned and said, "You're only thirty-five years old. How the fuck do you have arthritis?"

"Because I do, that's how," she snapped, then looked away again. "And why do you even care?" Her hand tightened on the heat pack, her knuckles blanching with the effort.

"Because you're my friend, Mia," Ollie snapped back, his frustration getting the better of him. "A little fact you seem to have forgotten." He shook his head. "I don't care how long it's been since we spoke last, you will always be my best friend. I will always want to know what's going on with you. So stop being so bloody stubborn and let me in. Like you used to."

"Don't tell me what to do," she snarled.

Oliver's lips pulled back from his teeth in a snarl of his own, and he hissed out a frustrated breath. "Let me in, Mia."

"You don't want me to do that," she said. "Not really."

Turning his body to face her, he said, "Yeah, actually, I do."

"No," she said more forcefully, looking sideways at him. "You don't. Because you won't like what you find there." Then she let out a breath and seemed to fold in on herself, her shoulders slumping and her head falling so far forwards that her chin almost rested on her chest. "I'm not the same girl you used to know, Ollie. I'm...."

"What?"

She lifted her head and stared out over the garden, then straightened her spine and hardened her voice. "Broken."

He shouldn't have been surprised by her attitude, not after the previous night. He'd seen how much it pained her to not be able to do something as simple as walk up a flight of stairs without help. Seen how she'd glared at the walking stick in her room when he'd woken her up that morning. Mia wasn't just stubborn, she was proud too.

A challenging combination.

She'd spent her whole life training to follow in her

father's footsteps and join the army, and had earned the nickname Major Mia long before she'd actually achieved the rank. The last time Ollie checked up on her, he'd been told she was on the fast track to colonel.

He'd been so proud of her, had always known she would achieve whatever she set her mind to, and he knew she still could.

No matter how broken she thought she might be.

"Better broken than dead," Ollie said, getting to his feet and taking the heat pack from Mia. "Now then, I'm going to reheat this pack for you, and you're going to tell me all about your medical discharge. And if we have time, which we will, you're also going to fill me in on what the fuck happened in the last eighteen years to make you so goddamn defeatist."

Eyes wide and mouth hanging open, Mia stared at Ollie as though she couldn't believe someone had spoken to her like that. At her rank, most people wouldn't dare. But Ollie wasn't most people, and Mia wasn't in the army anymore.

And she needed to get used to both of those facts. Fast.

7

Mia stared at Oliver's back as he stalked away from her, leaving her alone on the back deck with her anger and insecurities.

She had half a mind to storm off and leave him hanging, but her leg still twitched with the remnants of her last muscle spasm, and she didn't want to irritate it and set it off again. Besides, where would she go? She still wasn't sure she was up to the task of going home yet, and if hiding from Ollie was the goal, then skulking back to her bedroom was pointless since he'd put her in the one right beside his.

Finding her would not be difficult.

When he'd brought her to The Forge the previous night, they'd both been tired and cranky. Mia because she was in pain, and Ollie because he'd carried Mia on his back for the twenty-minute walk home, which included trudging uphill through thick scrubland.

He would have made a fine soldier.

She hadn't missed the way his thighs had quivered when he'd finally put her down, the muscles dancing under the denim of his jeans, undoubtedly fuelled by dehydration and lactic acid. Not that she'd been staring at his thighs in particular, comparing their current muscularity with the leanness of his youth.

Oliver Bennett's thighs were none of her business, and neither was what he did with them, or with whom.

Because they were friends.

Even after all this time, he still saw them as best friends. Which meant he didn't see her as anything else.

Fuck.

Mia sighed softly, then laughed at herself. "What did you expect? Idiot." Of course Ollie only saw them as friends. When had she ever given him the impression she'd wanted to be anything but?

Well, except for that one time.

And she'd fucked that up good and proper, hadn't she?

Ollie reappeared and handed her the heat pack. "Here you go," he said, sitting beside her. "Now tell me, it's not just arthritis, is it?"

"What do you want me to say, Ollie?" she said, reapplying the heat to her thigh. "For the last eighteen years, I've pushed my body beyond its limits and all so I could prove to every Tom, Dick and Harry that I had what it takes to be in charge of the men and women who defend our country. All so I could prove my lack of a penis meant I wasn't lacking anywhere else."

She scrubbed her free hand over her forehead and

sighed quietly. "After a while it takes its toll. I didn't even know I had arthritis until I put my back out last year. I slipped a disc and it impinged some nerves."

"And that's what's causing the muscle spasms?"

She nodded. "At my last check-up they told me the arthritis is getting worse in my lower spine, and my right hip is basically fucked. They strongly recommended I retire and find something less strenuous to do. I put in for my discharge the next day." She turned to look at Oliver, and added, "And it's not defeatist to accept reality. Circumstances change. I've learned to change with them."

"That's a very positive attitude," Ollie said, surprising her a little.

She frowned at the compliment. "Thank you."

"And doesn't sound at all like something a broken person would say."

She glared at him again. "Don't you have work to do?"

Oliver stretched his long legs out in front of him and knitted his fingers together, resting them on his taut stomach. "Probably."

Mia waited for him to get up but when he didn't make a move, she said, "Well, shouldn't you go do that, then?"

He smoothed one hand over his beard like he was stroking a cat. "Nah. The upside to being self-employed. I can do what I like, when I like. Especially on a Saturday."

"That seems... inefficient."

Ollie chuckled. "You'd be surprised. Besides, I thought you invited me to join you."

She blinked at him. "What?" *What is he talking about?*

"Pilates. I thought you said I should join you."

Ohh... that. "I thought you said no way."

"A man can change his mind."

Mia snorted. "Not in my experience, but if you say so."

Turning his head to grin at her, Ollie said, "Was that sass I just heard? Is Major Mia relaxed enough to throw down some sass?"

"Major Mia is relaxed enough to kick your arse, Bennett."

Ollie shook his head, feigning disappointment. "You know what I said I'd do if you called me Bennett again, sweetling." An evil grin spread across his handsome face, and he wiggled his fingers. "Prepare to be tickled."

Oh shit. "Don't you fucking dare!"

Heat pack forgotten, Mia leapt to her feet and tried to run, but Ollie and his long damn limbs caught her before she'd even reached the edge of the timber deck and took her to the ground. What ensued once he had his hands on her could only be described as a tickling frenzy.

His hands were everywhere.

Every. Where.

Her ribs, her stomach, her thighs, her back, behind her knees, under her feet, under her arms, on her breasts—

Her shrieks of laughter were cut off by a gasp and a sudden tightness in her belly, a pulsing warmth between her legs. Or maybe that was Ollie. Because Mia was pretty damn sure that was an erection she felt pressed between her thighs. Just like she was sure his breathing had matched hers, heavy and expectant.

Mia swallowed thickly. "Ollie...," she murmured, then licked her lips.

But he was on his feet and helping her get to hers before her brain could even begin to process what was happening. "Did I hurt you?"

"No, I'm okay," she said, smiling to hide her disappointment as she straightened her clothes and dusted herself off.

"I should get back to work," he said, thumbing over his shoulder at the forge as he backed away from her, stumbling a little as he stepped off the edge of the deck. "Do you need anything else before I go?" He seemed to stare at her mouth for a moment before clarifying, "For your... ah... leg?"

She shook her head. "No, I'm good. All stretched out, thanks."

"Good. That's... good." Without another word, he turned away and strode back into the dark of the forge, then kept his back to her as he did whatever the hell it was he did in there. Playing with literal fire.

"Good," Mia murmured, standing there watching him, rubbing her thigh and wondering what the hell had just happened. "Yep. All good."

Pain made Mia cranky at the best of times, but the realisation she'd been friend-zoned—again—by the only man she'd ever truly loved had kicked her irritation up a few notches.

And she wasn't even sure why.

Yeah, she'd loved Oliver Bennett—as a seventeen-year-old kid. Mia had gotten over him a long fucking time ago.

Hadn't she?

Wasn't that why she'd agreed to marry someone else, because she was well and truly over Ollie Bennett? Of course, that didn't explain why she'd broken off that engagement, or why she was even having these reckless thoughts.

It didn't matter. None of it did. She didn't come home to hook up with her teenage crush. She came home because...

Because she had nowhere else to go.

Eighteen years as an officer in the military—a female officer—didn't win her as many friends as her non-commissioned counterparts. She'd watched them form bonds with their diggers she'd known she could never have.

To maintain the chain of command, she'd held herself apart from those under her care. Because that's what they were, hers to care for. To keep safe. If that meant sacrificing her social life, then so be it.

It was a small price to pay.

But she wasn't an officer now. She had no one left to care for.

With that final depressing thought, she turned on her heel, swiped the heat pack off the deck, and strode back inside. Her body coursed with energy and sticky emotions she'd rather ignore, and sitting around pining for a man who was never going to see her as anything but a friend had never been her style.

After a quick shower, Mia pulled on a fresh pair of jeans and a T-shirt, grabbed her keys, and did what she'd failed to do the night before.

She went home.

8

Mia pulled into the driveway of Someday and cut the engine. The old house looked so different in the light of day and not at all like the impenetrable monolith it had felt like the night before.

Built in the typical Queenslander style of its day, the weatherboard box stood tall and proud on thick timber stumps with a wide veranda wrapped around it on all four sides, sash windows, and an old tin roof that could amplify the noise of a simple rainstorm until it sounded like the whole world was crashing down around you.

The old white paint was flaking off everything, and the gutters drooped to the point of being useless. The veranda railing was broken in several places and gone completely from the front stairs, and the gravel driveway and garden paths were so riddled with weeds it was hard to pick them out against the grass surrounding them.

Leaning forwards, she rested her forearms on the top of the steering wheel and stared at the yard. The grass was long and lush and in desperate need of a mow, and the pink and purple bougainvillea were in full flower, adding a splash of colour to the verdant landscape in front of her.

When she opened the door and stepped out of the car, the rich scent of sun-warmed frangipanis and gardenias hit her like a truck; even if she'd wanted to, she couldn't have stopped the smile that spread across her face.

Closing her eyes, she breathed deeply, sucking down the wondrous smells of her childhood, of clean air and damp earth and sunshine.

For the first time since she'd arrived in town, all the tension ebbed out of her and she felt the peace that only comes from going home. Home to a place she knew she belonged. Her earlier admission that she'd had nowhere else to go exposed itself for the lie it was. She had plenty of places she could go if she chose to, but none that lived in her blood, in her heart as much as Someday.

Certainly none that afforded her a challenge she actually looked forward to.

She hadn't felt like that in the longest time—excited, eager—and she knew then, truly knew she'd made the right decision by discharging. The timing fit.

And it felt good knowing she was going to help people.

She felt good.

At least she did until a sleek black car with a realtor

sign stuck on the side of it pulled up in front of the house.

Mia narrowed her gaze behind her sunglasses and assumed her best "Don't fuck with me" face as she watched a man in a slim-fit suit exit the car and stride towards her like his dick was leading the charge.

"What the hell does this guy want?" she muttered under her breath.

"Good morning," he called out, his tanned face almost split in half by the most disingenuous smile Mia had ever seen in her life. And she'd been forced to dine with several politicians throughout the course of her career, so the bar was set pretty high in that arena.

"Hello," she replied, keeping her tone on the icy side of neutral. "Are you lost?"

As he walked closer, the man extended his hand, but Mia didn't shake it. Rather she stood there with her arms folded across her chest and stared at him until he dropped his arm to his side. One of the advantages to being almost six feet tall was that men of a similar height tended to find her intimidating and didn't push their luck.

Unlike the outrageously tall Oliver Bennett, who'd easily and unapologetically thrown her to the ground and tickled her like he had when they were in school.

But now probably wasn't the best time to be thinking about that. Actually, there was no good time to think about Ollie pinning her down and touching her everywhere after declaring her the Queen of Friendsville.

That path led nowhere good.

"Not lost, no. I'm Greg Wheeler from Wheeler Realty. Are you the owner of this property?"

One brow hitched above her sunglasses. "Why?"

Wheeler laughed, as if he found Mia's obvious distrust of him amusing. "I have a buyer who is very interested in acquiring this property," he said, smiling up at the house. "It's been vacant for so long we weren't sure it hadn't been abandoned."

One only had to look at the freshly swept verandas and distinct lack of cobwebs clinging to the outside of the house to know that simply wasn't true. If only Ollie had weeded the pathways as a part of his maintenance routine. Mia hated weeding. "Is that so?"

The realtor's smile tightened, and if she didn't know any better, she'd say the brevity of her answers was beginning to piss the guy off. His words were definitely sharper when he said, "I assure you, my buyer is willing to pay you a very fair price for the land."

"Just the land?"

Mia had recently had the property evaluated because she'd wanted to know exactly how much it was going to cost for repairs and renovations. But that also meant she knew approximately what Someday was worth.

Spoiler alert: a fucking lot.

"Million-dollar views," the official property valuer had said. "Literally."

The report also told her most of that value was in the land, not the house.

Wheeler didn't answer her, just handed her a business card with $385,000 scribbled on the back of it. Mia wasn't sure if she should laugh at his audacity or punch him in the face.

"And this figure is deemed fair for a property like this one?" she asked, trying for all she was worth to sound as ignorant as he obviously thought she was.

"For a one-acre block and a house that needs extensive renovations, yes, that's a very fair and, may I say, a very serious offer. My buyer is eager to make a deal."

No shit, Sherlock. But a deal for whom? Not her. Not at that price.

Looking down at the business card again, Mia rolled her lips between her teeth, if only to stop herself from laughing at Wheeler's extraordinary restraint. How the man was keeping a straight face while trying to pass off this lowball insult as the deal of the century was truly baffling.

Eventually she let out a small sigh and shook her head. "I'm sorry you came all this way for nothing, Mr Wheeler, but the property isn't for sale."

He threw her another phony smile. "Everything's for sale for the right price, Miss... I'm sorry, I didn't catch your name."

"No, you didn't. Good day, Mr Wheeler," she said, handing him back his business card.

He didn't take it. "Keep it. In case you have a change of heart. I hope to hear from you soon."

A change of heart? Seriously? Like she was the heartless one, depriving some cheapskate arsehole the privilege of living in her childhood home? The one she had no intension of selling no matter what it was worth.

She had plans for good ol' Someday.

Plans she hoped her parents would be proud of.

9

Mia's progress up the front stairs ran much more smoothly than the night before, even without the handrail for support. Turned out the walking stick wasn't the worst idea in the world. Who knew?

Pushing the front door open once she'd unlocked it, however, was still a challenge.

It was the first time she'd been home since her mother's funeral. The first time she knew for certain Louisa wouldn't be there to greet her, and not because she was out back in the garden or had gone to the shops to pick up something for dinner.

She was gone.

Forever.

And Mia's world felt smaller for the loss.

"Come on, Caldwell," she whispered. "You've got this." Taking a deep breath, she opened the door and stepped through.

The first thing that hit her was a wave of sadness. The second was a barrage of happy memories that swept the sadness aside and propelled her down the wide hallway.

"Hey, Mum. I'm home," she said, running her hand over the family photographs hanging in the hall. "Hi, Dad," she added, stopping to stare at a picture of her and the colonel, marching proudly together at an ANZAC Day parade.

The last one her father ever attended.

He'd died the following year, drowned while helping some idiot escape his 4WD after attempting to cross a bridge in rising flood waters. That was fifteen years ago. Didn't make the sting of his loss any easier to bear.

Reaching the back of the house, she drew aside the curtains, exposing the French doors that led to the rear veranda. Using the new keys Oliver had given her the night before, she unlocked the doors and pushed them wide open, then repeated the process for every door and window in every room, releasing the stale air trapped in the house and letting in the fresh omnipresent scent of the nearby rainforests.

Kinda like a domestic version of "Inhale the good shit, exhale the bullshit."

What Mia hadn't anticipated was finding most of her family's belongings already packed up in boxes, labelled and stacked neatly in the main room of the house, the furniture covered in dust sheets.

She'd been dreading what she'd find when she finally

came home again. Her father may have preferred a Spartan lifestyle but her mother never met a crafting supply she didn't like, and hoarded every scrap of paper, fabric and cardboard that crossed her path for future uses that never materialised.

Did Ollie do all of this?

The distinct lack of grime throughout the house did not escape her notice either, nor did the new kettle she discovered on the kitchen bench sitting next to a box of her favourite brand of tea bags, a jar of honey, three lemons and her father's flask.

He found it.

When Ollie hadn't said anything about it at breakfast, or later outside, she'd thought maybe he hadn't been able to find it. Or maybe he hadn't even looked.

She should have known better.

Oliver always kept his word. Always had. Probably always would.

And he'd never been one to brag, so of course he hadn't said anything about it.

Mia mentally slapped herself for jumping to conclusions. She'd spent the last eighteen years living in a world where everything had a double meaning, everyone had a secret agenda, and nothing and no one could be taken at face value.

She'd forgotten what it felt like to have someone do something for her without the expectation of getting something in return.

As for the tea....

How could he possibly remember something as insignificant as how she liked her tea? Her ex couldn't even remember not to put milk in it. Because according to him, tea without milk was unnatural.

After making herself a cup of unnatural tea, Mia wandered out to the veranda. She stared out over the valley to the mountains beyond, traced her gaze over their jagged edges and watched them change colour from green to grey and back again as the clouds above cast shadows that undulated across their surface.

She'd always loved sitting out there, at the back of the house where it was quiet and the prying eyes of their neighbours couldn't reach.

Before her mother passed, the back veranda had always been used as a sort of outdoor lounge room. The whole area had been filled with potted plants, ferns and African violets and such, and a collection of wicker chairs had surrounded a matching coffee table with a glass top.

Mia had always hated that table. Every time she set her mug down, it made an awful clunking sound that made her think either the table or the mug was about to shatter. The chairs were comfy though, even if they were upholstered in the most garish palm frond fabric her mother could find. Louisa thought it added to the trop-ical nature of their home. Mia and the colonel had agreed letting her mother think that would be best for all parties involved.

"Happy wife, happy life," her father used to whisper to her before praising his wife's design choices, to which her mother would roll her eyes.

Louisa had always known what her husband was up to and played along. Sometimes Mia thought her mother made deliberately ghastly decisions just to stir the man up and get a reaction out of him. That reaction generally being a smack on her arse as he walked past her and a lot of noise coming from their bedroom at night, which Mia had drowned out with headphones and loud music.

Still, it was kinda romantic.

Certainly more romantic than anything any of her boyfriends had ever done for her.

As she leaned against the railing of the now empty veranda, Mia sipped her tea and considered her plans for the house and grounds. Like the house, the yard was in much better shape than she'd expected, and she wondered if Ollie's maintenance had extended to the gardens.

After meandering through the house for almost an hour, running through her mental to-do list and figuring out what she needed and how she was going to get it, Mia began feeling weary. She needed to rest. So she washed her mug and locked up the house, then slowly ambled down the front stairs, adding "build a ramp" to her to-do list.

Before climbing back into her car, she gave a few more moments of thought to the name of the property.

Someday.

Her parents had named it that because *someday* they'd planned to turn it into their dream home, but that day had never come, and Mia wasn't a dream home kind of girl.

She was, however, a veteran, and there were plenty of people just like her who needed a quiet place they could visit, a safe place where they could get out of their own damn heads and begin to heal.

A place they could start planning their very own someday.

10

Ollie hung up his leather apron, rolled his shoulders, and worked out the kinks in his neck. His muscles ached like a sonofabitch and it was only midday. *Nothing a good long soak in an Epsom salt bath won't fix.*

Standing back, he stared at the ornate driveway gate he was building. It was ugly as fuck, but he didn't design it and he didn't have to live with it, so... whatever. He'd tried steering his client towards something more classic in style, but she'd been adamant this monstrosity was what she truly wanted. And giving his clients what they wanted was how he'd managed to make a living from his craft. Word of mouth was his most effective advertising tool, and happy clients loved to talk.

Of course, it didn't hurt that he looked the way he did. More than one client—both male and female—had mentioned he looked like Thor. A fact he wasn't shy of flaunting if it meant turning a potential client into a return customer. His natural combination of looks and charm won most people over.

Not that he'd always been that way.

Not many people would guess he'd been a shy kid, lacking in confidence and bullied at school because of his extreme height and slim build.

At least until a certain army brat moved to town and beat the shit out of his tormentors on his behalf.

He couldn't believe Abby had brought that up at breakfast. *Thanks, sis!* He could have happily forgotten that day had ever existed, but Abby had always been a little awestruck by Mia, and understandably so.

She was pretty amazing.

Melville's Cross was so small, it didn't have a high school of its own, so the kids had to take the bus to the larger coastal townships. Ollie and Mia both attended one of the more prestigious schools, the type where the uniform included a mandatory blazer with an ornate crest stitched into the pocket.

Oliver had seen the Caldwells around town a few times during the summer holidays but hadn't actually met Mia until their first day of high school, when she'd sat beside him on the bus.

On purpose.

"Is this seat taken?" she'd asked after walking straight past a dozen empty seats.

Ollie had shaken his head, then scooched over, sitting as close to the window as possible so he wouldn't accidentally touch her.

Back then the girls didn't appreciate what Ollie was capable of, didn't know how much pleasure a pair of big, callused hands could wreak on their soft skin. Of course, Ollie wasn't exactly aware of his skills at that age either, so he couldn't totally blame them for keeping their distance.

Especially from someone they'd been told was to be avoided at all costs, no matter how ridiculous it might have seemed to anyone who actually knew him or his family. But prejudice died a slow death in a small town like Melville's Cross, and there were more than a few good citizens ever willing to put Oliver and his siblings in their place should they get the chance.

Arseholes.

But apparently Mia didn't get that memo and thought nothing of sitting next to him. As if he was a normal person and not one of Ulysses Bennett's bastard children.

"I'm Emilia, by the way," she'd said, and stuck out her hand. "Emilia Caldwell. But you can call me Mia. What's your name?"

"Ollie," he'd replied, shaking her hand. Then he'd swallowed hard before adding, "Bennett." Then he'd sat as stiff as a board, waiting for her to groan in disgust and move to a different seat, but when she didn't, he'd felt the need to tell her she should.

She'd looked up at him with doubt and confusion, the way his sister did when he told her there was no more ice cream. Like she didn't quite believe he was being serious. "Why?"

But he was very serious. "If you sit with me, the other kids will pick on you."

A slow smile had spread across her face as she'd looked up at him, her eyes bright and mischievous, and Ollie was smitten. No one had ever smiled at him like that before. Like they saw him.

The real him.

He was pretty sure he'd blushed.

"Now I *know* I'm in the right seat," she'd said with confidence.

"What do you mean?"

"Well, we've only just met, but you're already worried about me. You care. I like people who care about others. And if the bullies don't like us being friends, they can suck it."

Her statement had made him laugh out loud—hell, it still made him smile remembering how officious she was for a twelve-year-old—but it had also helped him relax, softened his rigid posture, and caused his leg to bump into hers. And he'd been quick to notice she hadn't flinched away as so many had before. They'd talked for the entire bus ride to school, and again on the ride home. And over the days and weeks and months, they'd forged a friendship Ollie had thought unbreakable.

They'd been the best of friends, had told each other everything, did everything together.

Even shared their first time together.

But just as he'd finally gotten up the courage to tell her how he felt, she'd left. Signed her life away and hopped on a bus headed for the military college in Canberra.

He'd been too late. Had missed his chance. And he hadn't heard from her since.

Oliver's mood soured.

Mia had always planned a career in the military, to follow in her father's footsteps. He'd known what she'd wanted from the day they'd met, had even helped her study and train, so it shouldn't have come as any great surprise when she'd left.

But she'd never said a damn thing about leaving him behind.

His hurt had ruled him for years after she left, and he'd made more than his fair share of stupid mistakes because of it.

Slept with more women than he cared to think about.

But sex was a temporary fix. It only gave him a momentary high before dropping him on his arse again, feeling even shittier than he had before. Worse than that was the fact it ate away at him, slowly but surely turning him into the thing people had always said he was.

Trash.

And when it wasn't women he wanted to fuck, it was women—one woman—he wanted to find. His mother. The woman who'd given him away the day he was born and never looked back.

What an absolute disaster that reunion had been.

It had taken him a couple of years but he'd finally tracked her down in Norway, the country of her birth.

Ollie didn't know what he'd hoped to find, but it wasn't the entitled drunken socialite who thought he was the sexy young thing she'd hired for the night. She'd sobered up real quick when he'd told her who he really was.

Then just as quickly disabused him of any notions he might have held that she was anything other than a cold, selfish bitch. "I never wanted you. I certainly never loved you. You were nothing more than a blip on my radar. The day your father took you away from me was the happiest day of my life. I have no son."

If Mia leaving him had been the knife in his heart, Grete's words had been the hand wrapped around the handle, forcing it deeper and giving it a sinister little twist at the end.

By the age of twenty-one, he'd been abandoned by the only girl he'd ever loved. And the ice queen formerly known as his mother had rejected him twice.

Was it any wonder he avoided relationships like the plague?

"Ollie, lunch," his sister called from the back door.

Keeping his back to her, he lifted his hand and waved in acknowledgement. "Be there in a sec," he called over his shoulder.

He didn't want her to see the anguish he was struggling to conceal. Abby was very protective of her brothers, Ollie in particular seeing as they were the closest in age. He didn't want her worrying about him, especially as there was nothing she could do to help.

Once he heard the screen door bang shut again, Ollie started towards the house, taking deep breaths as he went. He'd recently started seeing a therapist and the man was a big believer in the benefits of meditation, breathing exercises and being present in the now.

And he be damned if it didn't work.

His deep breaths helped him centre himself and dragged him from the dark well of his thoughts, and by the time he'd washed his hands and joined his family in the kitchen, he was just about ready to see Mia again.

11

Ollie reached for the salad bowl just as Mia entered the kitchen carrying a small white box. She was limping slightly even though she was using the hated walking stick, but when he moved to help her, she shook her head at him. She didn't want him making a fuss.

Gritting his teeth, he sat back down. *Stubborn woman.*

"Sorry I'm late," she said. "I popped into the patisserie and got chatting to Mary Melville." She opened the box before putting it on the table, then took the chair next to his. "Compliments of the chef."

"Raspberry friands," Wolf said, licking his lips as he stared at the tiny cakes. "That woman will be the death of me. Do you have any idea how much weight I've gained since moving to Melville's Cross?"

"If you're that worried about it, we could stay at your place in Sydney for a while," Abby suggested.

"Wouldn't help," Wolf said with a resigned sigh. "My

mother is as bad as Mary when it comes to feeding my sweet tooth."

Oliver chuckled at his future brother-in-law's first-world problem and passed the salad to Mia. "Thank you," she said quietly. Turning to look at him, she captured his gaze and smiled in a way that took his breath away. The last time he'd seen that smile was eighteen years ago. When he was inside her. "For the flask."

He hid his interest by grinning back. "You thought I forgot, didn't you?"

In truth, he'd gone back to look for the flask as soon as he'd gotten her settled in one of the spare bedrooms and told her to get some sleep. It had only taken him half an hour to find it. The sneaky little bugger was wedged good and tight between a tree root and the garden edging. It was a little banged up, but the engraving was undamaged. He'd managed to buff out the scratches without too much trouble.

He'd intended to tell her about it when he woke her up that morning, but then she'd thrown back the covers, revealing her toned body with those insanely long legs and perfect breasts.

Fuck. He could wax lyrical about those breasts.

His brain had stalled at the sight of her, and then it had flipped a switch and gone into overdrive and flooded his mind with memories of the one and only time she'd had those legs wrapped tightly around him as she came, screaming his name.

Okay, maybe not just once. It had been a wild afternoon.

His cock had twitched against his thigh, he'd licked his lips, and then Mia had started a conversation about camping and Ollie had completely forgotten to tell her he'd found her father's flask.

"I didn't think that at all," Mia protested, then lifted one shoulder in a half-hearted shrug. "Okay, I didn't think that for very long," she added, grinning. "But I've never been gladder to be proven wrong."

"What did Oliver forget this time?" Rafe asked before sinking his teeth into a chicken leg.

"Hey, you heard the woman," Ollie protested, frowning at his brother. "I didn't forget anything."

"I dropped my dad's flask last night when I was walking home from the cemetery and couldn't find it. It's not worth much, except for its sentimental value, but I was paranoid someone would find it and keep it. And Ollie promised he'd go back and look for it if I let him get me off—"

Jane sputtered and half choked. "Ollie promised to get you off?"

"Her leg, Janie," Ollie growled as everyone else snorted and chuckled behind their hands. "I got her off her bad leg." When his sister-in-law grinned wickedly at him like the imp she was, he rolled his eyes. "Jesus Christ. I can't wait until you pop out those babies so you can focus all your attention on them and stop being a pain in *my* arse."

"Really?" Jane said. "And here I thought you were just eager to have two more nieces to dote on." Then she let loose an exaggerated sigh, shook her head, and added, "I do hope Josie and Diana don't get jealous of their new cousins stealing away their favourite uncle's attention."

"Pretty sure Josie and Diana will be the first in line to offer their babysitting services," Abby said, then winked at Ollie. "Followed very closely by their favourite uncle."

Ollie chose to ignore his siblings and eat his lunch, knowing the second he was back in the forge he'd be doing a solid half hour of breathing exercises to make up for the fact he wasn't currently telling them all to go fuck themselves.

Of course he was a devoted uncle. The likelihood he was ever having kids of his own was slim to none, so he had to direct all that protective instinct somewhere.

"Who are Josie and Diana?" Mia asked.

"Charlie's twin girls. They'll be fourteen this year."

Mia started choking on her food and grabbed for her water glass. "Wait a second," she said after swallowing half the glass of water. "You're telling me Charlie—*Charlie*—has kids? Someone actually chose to procreate with that serial pest? On purpose?"

"Yep," Oliver said, grinning, then told Mia the tale of how Charlie became a father.

"So... he knocked up his lesbian best friend's bisexual lover because it was cheaper than IVF? Do I have that right?"

"Yep," Ollie said again.

Mia seemed to mull that over for a moment before nodding. "Well, I guess it's on brand for the Bennetts," she said, making the rest of the table laugh. "You've always been the most interesting family I know. And the most welcoming." Then she ducked her head and shifted in her seat. "Thank you for letting me stay here last night."

It wasn't instinct that had Ollie reaching for her hand and giving it a squeeze. It was need. A powerful need to touch her again. "You're welcome to stay at The Forge for as long as you like."

She could stay forever, if she wanted to.

12

Mia couldn't remember the last time she'd had a home-cooked meal with friends, and now she'd had two in one day.

No one put out a spread better than Abby and Jane. She'd known them since she was twelve and they were nine, but even back then they were the ones in charge of the kitchen.

As an only child, Mia had been endlessly fascinated by the Bennetts. There were just so many of them, nine in all, plus two nieces—the daughters of the two eldest brothers—who were of a similar age to Abby.

Every day had been an adventure at The Forge.

There was always something to do or learn, and always someone willing to teach her new tricks. She'd had painting lessons from Ulysses, their dad. Learned how to strike cuttings from the garden from Toby, Charlie's twin brother. And even Charlie himself, pain in the arse that he was, had taught her all about football. A skill that had come in infinitely handy when it came to breaking the ice within a new unit.

She'd missed that. The easy camaraderie. The unconditional love. So when Ollie said she could stay as long as she liked, she said, "Okay." Then she cleared her throat and added, "Thank you."

"Did you look at the house this morning?" Rafe asked her.

Rafe was the only member of the Bennett family who didn't work in the arts. He was a family lawyer, and a damn fine one too. He'd been her mother's lawyer for about five years before she'd passed away, and he'd done everything in his power to make everything that came after her death as painless as possible for Mia. He was a good man, and she had a hunch he was going to be a great dad.

"Yes I did. Even made it all the way inside this time."

"And what did you think?"

Mia's brow pinched. "I think it needs a lot of work and will cost me a shitload of money. I also think for an almost empty house, it was very clean." Oliver shifted beside her but avoided her gaze. "I owe a debt to whomever packed up everything and looked after the place for me," she said, reaching for Oliver's hand again. "And also for the tea."

When he looked up at her, she saw in his beautiful blue eyes the boy she'd known all those years ago. The sweet, kind, gentle boy she'd fallen for.

The boy she'd almost given up everything for.

Only now, mixed in with all that sweet, was an over-abundance of sexy.

It didn't help that Ollie had the most seductive smile she'd ever laid eyes on. *When did he learn to smile like that?* Or that he now sported the body of a Norse god, with muscles on his muscles and an arse so perfectly formed she wanted nothing more than to smack it and watch it ripple. Maybe bite it.

Definitely bite it.

Actually, there were few parts of Oliver Bennett she wouldn't mind sinking her teeth into.

But just as her imagination started running wild, just as she noticed Ollie's gaze flick to her lips and back, Wolf ruined the moment by leaning towards Abby and whispering none too quietly, "Is it just me, or did they used to fuck?"

Ollie snapped his head around and levelled a glare at his sister's lover. "Fuck—and I cannot stress this enough —off."

Always the protector.

Even when she didn't deserve it.

Wolf draped his arm over the back of Abby's chair and laughed. "Just curious, is all."

"Well the only thing I'm curious about is what Mia intends to do with Someday," Abby said, nudging her lover with her elbow.

"Good question," Rafe said. "That's why Louisa asked us to pack up the house for you as much as possible. She wanted you to be able to do whatever it was you wanted to do without having to sift through, and I quote, 'decades of crap' first."

Mia laughed. "That sounds exactly like something Mum would say."

Rafe continued, "She said she didn't know what plans you had for the future, but whether you wanted to renovate the house or sell it, she wanted you to be able to start the next phase of your life as soon as possible."

Mia set her cutlery down and sat back in her chair. "Funny you should mention selling the house," she began, "because about five seconds after I pulled up in the driveway, some real estate guy showed up and told me he had a buyer already lined up, then offered me an insultingly small sum of money."

Abby, Wolf and Jane all voiced their shock and outrage, but she couldn't miss the look shared by Rafe and Oliver. They didn't seem shocked by her news at all.

"What?" she asked them. "What do you know?"

Oliver ran his tongue over his teeth then stared at his older brother. "You want to tell them or should I...?"

Rafe leaned forwards, resting his elbows on the table and sighed heavily. "That's not the first time someone approached with an offer to buy the place." He looked at Mia. "Was his name Wheeler?"

"Yes," she said, reaching into her pocket for the business card. She handed it to Rafe. "Greg Wheeler."

When he turned the card over and saw the number on the back, he laughed and shook his head, then showed the number to Ollie.

"For fuck's sake," Ollie muttered.

"What?" Mia demanded.

"That's almost half what he offered us six months ago," Ollie said.

"What? Why are we only just hearing about this?" Jane demanded.

Rafe cocked one brow as he stared down his wife. "You mean, why didn't I tell you something that was none of your business even though we weren't dating and you were engaged to another man and I wasn't speaking to you?"

Jane scowled and pointed at Oliver. "But he wasn't."

Ollie snorted. "Don't drag me into this."

"Neither of you told me, either," Abby reminded them, staring at her brothers with wide eyes.

"Honestly, we didn't think it was that big of a deal," Ollie said. "A big storm had come through and knocked down a few branches, so we spent the weekend cleaning up."

"Toby brought his big wood chipper up from Brisbane," Rafe said. "So I guess it could have looked like we were getting the place ready to sell. But when this Wheeler bloke showed up, all my worst lawyer instincts went on high alert. There was just something off about the guy."

"I know what you mean," Mia said. "He smiled too damn much for starters, and he didn't seem happy when I said I had no intention of selling."

"I bet. After our encounter with him, I did some digging. Turns out his buyer is a husband and wife team with a history of harassing people until they either agree to sell or get a restraining order.

"These people buy up premium land in small towns on the cheap, then flog it off to developers looking to build boutique hotels and supermarket chains. The chain stores move in, small local businesses go under, and slowly but surely the town dynamic shifts. Things that used to make a town unique vanish, tourism suffers, land values drop."

Rafe scrubbed his hand through his hair. "Thankfully, most of the small hinterland towns are too far away from the beaches to be of much value to the hotels hoping to cash in on that market. But Melville's Cross backs onto a national rainforest, and Someday has some of the best views in town, looking out over the valley and mountain ranges."

He shook his head. "Nothing these people are doing is illegal, so I don't know what I can do to stop it from happening here. Eventually someone is going to take this guy up on his offer."

"Well I know what I can do," Mia said. She waited until she had everyone's attention before continuing. "I'm turning Someday into a veteran's retreat. If scores of big, scary soldiers in holiday mode don't keep these arseholes away, I don't know what will."

13

"I have to get back to work," Oliver said as he finished his lunch. Then he turned to Mia. "I don't suppose you'd like to give me a hand?"

"Sure. What are we doing?"

"Putting rivets in the world's ugliest gate."

Mia burst out laughing. The sound of it wrapped around him and made his cock twitch.

"He's not kidding," Abby said, grinning. "It's hideous." Then to him she added, "I still can't believe you couldn't talk her out of it."

Mia's gaze snapped to his. "Who?" she said, the word snapping out of her.

She almost sounded possessive.

Jealous, sweetling?

His heart rate kicked up at the idea so he tested the waters further. "My client, Mrs Williams. I tried to sway her towards something more conventional but she seems oddly immune to my charms."

Mia's eyes narrowed. "And which charms would those be?"

"You mean you're *not* intimately acquainted with Oliver's charms?" Wolf said, his face a perfect picture of confusion.

Ollie grabbed Mia's hand and tugged her towards the door before he turned his friend's face into the perfect picture of a broken nose and a black eye.

The big man grinned at him as they exited the kitchen. "Was it something I said?" he called after them.

As he stalked across the backyard to the forge, practically dragging Mia behind him, she asked, "Is he always like that?"

"Wolf? Not usually. Usually he's a pretty good guy."

"Usually?"

"Hmm." Ollie's lips twisted and he let go of Mia's hand. "He's just being a shit-stirrer because—"

Mia raised an eyebrow at his sudden silence. "Because why?"

Yeah, why was Wolf stirring up so much trouble?

Ollie pressed his palms against the forge doors, closed his eyes and shook his head. He knew why. He also knew no amount of deep breathing was going to help him get through what he was about to do, so he opened his eyes again, and grumbled over his shoulder, "Because he knows how much I want to fuck you."

It was true. He did. Because Ollie had told him one night, months ago, when they were half-drunk on his father's home brew. Wolf had asked him why he hadn't settled down yet, and Ollie had spilled his guts about the one that got away.

There had been other women in his life—too many to count—but none he'd ever shared any sort of meaningful connection with.

None except Mia.

He couldn't explain why but he still felt a pull towards her, stronger than anything he'd ever known. Like supercharged magnets.

The attraction was intense.

Laying her hand on his back, Mia said, "Why does Wolf know that?"

The warmth of her hand soaked through his T-shirt and into his flesh. Her touch was gentle, yet he knew she wasn't always that way. Mia could be demanding, challenging. She was born to take charge but wielded her power with care.

"Oliver, look at me."

Her stern command sent a shiver through his big body, filling him with a joy, a serenity he hadn't felt in almost two decades. It was a feeling he never thought he'd feel again and he almost laughed out loud at the return of it, bewildered by the realisation it had never really left him.

He'd tried to find someone he could share that part of himself with, but in all the years, and all the women, no one could make him submit.

No one except her.

Slowly he turned to face her. "Yes, sweetling?"

She lifted her chin and locked her gaze with his.

"Why does Wolf know you want to fuck me? Why does he know anything about me at all?"

"Because I told him about you, how I feel about you. How much I missed you."

"And?"

Ollie smiled as he realised everything he'd told Wolf that night was true. He also realised it wasn't prudent to tell Mia *everything* he'd told Wolf.

He didn't want to scare her off again. Not now that she was finally back.

"And that you're the only woman who ever brought me to my knees." When she broke eye-contact, he added quickly, "And you can't tell me you're not interested. That you haven't noticed this pull between us. I see the way you look at me, Mia. I know you feel it, too."

Taking a chance, he grabbed her hand and pulled her body into his, slid his arms around her waist and cupped her arse, held her to him. Pressed his growing erection against her belly.

"I definitely feel something," she murmured, rocking her hips against his cock, making him harder. "But we've gone from zero to sixty in the blink of an eye," she said, pushing out of his embrace. "Ollie, we haven't seen each other since we were kids, and I know it feels like everything's the same between us, but it isn't. We're not the same people we were back then."

"I know that, but I also know what I feel is real." Anchoring his hands on his hips, he dropped his head forwards and sighed. "Mia, I've tried to forget you. Fuck knows, I've tried." He looked up from under the veil of his lashes and caught her gaze. "But no one, not a single woman in the last eighteen years has ever made me feel the way you do."

To prove his point he lowered himself to his knees and stared up at her.

His name escaped her on a shuddering gasp. "Ollie...."

"If you truly feel nothing for me, tell me now and I'll never mention it again." His heart cracked even thinking the words, let alone saying them out loud. "We'll go back to the way things were. We'll go back to being just friends."

But then a slow smile spread across her face and she stared at him the way she used, like he was an overgrown puppy she didn't know what to do with. That's when he knew for sure.

He wasn't alone in this.

"I never said I didn't feel it," she said, and reached out to unfasten his man-bun, ran her fingers through his long hair. He leaned into her touch. It felt so good. "Only that we're moving too fast." She sighed softly. "I've missed you too. I've missed my friend."

"Only your friend?"

Sinking her teeth into her bottom lip, she frowned, but it wasn't aimed at him. "One thing I've learned over time, contrary to popular belief, is that friends *can* be lovers, and Ollie, I don't just mean friends with benefits." She continued playing with his hair, as though it gave her something to focus on while she sorted through her thoughts. She used to do the same thing when they were teens, and he would rest his head in her lap. "I think the main reason I broke off my engagement—"

Wait, what? "You were engaged?" *Why didn't I know that?*

"Yes. After mum passed away I finally agreed to marry my boyfriend, but I broke it off a month later." She shook her head and huffed a laugh. "There'd always been something missing between us, something I thought getting married would fix. But after attending a friend's wedding, after I saw what she shared with her husband, I finally understood."

"Understood what?"

"The main reason I broke it off with Josh was because we weren't friends. Outside of the bedroom, we had nothing to talk about. It wasn't that we had nothing in common, because we did, but there was a disconnect between us. We may as well have led separate lives for all we truly knew about each other." She stared down at him again, her gaze narrowed under a stern brow. "For instance, what's my favourite colour?"

"You don't have one," Ollie said, smiling up at her. "It wouldn't be fair to all the other colours."

Tears welled in Mia's eyes, even as she smiled, too. Ollie wanted to reach up and wipe her tears away, but kept his hands firmly by his side. He would wait until she was ready for his touch.

"What's my favourite food?"

"Barbeque beef ribs with blue cheese sauce." He laughed. "Jane cooked it once for a family barbie and you declared it was the best thing you'd ever put in your mouth."

"My ex didn't know any of that. And he didn't want to know. He used to say we were a power couple, both working our way to the top, but the truth was we were only together because it was convenient. I honestly couldn't tell you what his favourite anything is either. Neither of us cared about that stuff because we weren't friends."

Levering himself to his feet, Ollie cupped Mia's face. Stroked his thumbs over the soft curve of her cheeks and wiped away the silent tears tracking down her face. "What's my favourite colour?"

"Blue," she said, then hiccoughed a laugh. "The other colours can all suck it."

Ollie grinned and asked, "My favourite food?"

"Chilli mud crab."

"Coke or Pepsi?" he asked.

"Coke. Duh. Peanut butter or Nutella?"

"Both at the same time, but only if the peanut butter is smooth. If it's just peanut butter, you prefer crunchy." Gently, he tilted her face higher, leaned his forehead against hers and breathed her in. She smelled like frangipanis. "Did you really think I'd forget how you take your tea?" Wrapping his arms around her, he pulled Mia close, sighed softly, content when she did the same.

"I should have known better, huh?"

"Yes, you should have," he teased, then leaned back so he could look at her again. "So, what exactly have we decided here?"

"That friendship is a good foundation for a relationship," Mia said with a decisive nod of her head.

"And we agree that we are still best friends?"

"Obviously."

"Then can we also agree to skip over any more awkwardness and just start having a relationship already?"

Mia chuckled. "I'd forgotten how bossy you can be when you really want something."

Ollie leaned down and brushed his lips over hers in the barest of kisses. "I'm not bossy, I'm assertive. Besides, you know as well as I do, you can wrap me around your little finger anytime you wish. All you have to do is say the word. You do remember the word, don't you sweetling?"

Instead of answering him, Mia said, "I think you should take me out on a date. If you want a relationship, I want some romance."

"Hmm, a date you say? And what should we do about all this sexual tension?"

He leaned down to kiss her but she slid her fingers between their lips and gently pushed him back. "Well," she hedged, her mouth kicking up at the corners in a sexy little grin. "Play your cards right and I might be tempted to put out on the first date."

Cupping her arse, he yanked her against him again and pressed his now rock hard cock between her thighs.

"Excellent. I'll pick you up at six." Then he let her go and grabbed his leather apron, but not before noticing the spark of anticipation in her eyes. "Now then," he said, handing Mia a pair of heavy leather gloves, "help me with the fucking flamingos on this godawful gate."

14

Mia checked the time as she paced back and forth by the bed in her room. The room Oliver had put her in. The one right beside his.

It was almost six o'clock.

She turned to stare at the wall that separated them. Was he in there now? Was he dressed? Was he naked? Was he as nervous as she was? Was he going to wear another one of those sexy T-shirts that showed off his biceps to perfection and made her mouth go dry?

Is it hot in here?

What was she thinking?

This was so not a good idea. Yes, she'd been disappointed after their brief chat in the morning when she'd thought he only wanted to be friends again. And yes, she should be over the moon about how completely and utterly wrong she'd been.

But what if they fucked it up?

What if she was wrong about being friends *and* lovers? What if they tried the lovers part and screwed up the friends part?

What if she lost Oliver, truly lost him?

She wouldn't be able to blame it on the stupidity of youth this time, because this time they were both old enough to know exactly what they were getting in to.

Okay, so maybe she hadn't let go of certain things from their past as much as she'd thought. Maybe she'd just kinda swept them under the proverbial carpet where they'd had time to grow claws and fangs and plot revenge for being ignored for so long.

It's definitely hot it here.

Mia grabbed a magazine off the small desk near the window and fanned herself with it. It was the middle of summer after all, and the humidity was insane, but it was her anxiety that was causing her to sweat. And the last thing she needed on a date was pit stains. *Maybe I should change.*

Before she even finished the thought, a knock sounded at the door, then swung open to reveal Oliver.

Her friend.

Her date.

Her date who was dressed in soft looking denim that hugged his muscular thighs, leather boots and a button up shirt that revealed his toned, tanned forearms and that intriguing tattoo.

Her anxiety melted away at the drop dead gorgeous sight of him. Even his beard looked more groomed than usual, and instead of the man-bun, his hair was pulled back in one long, thick braid.

It was surprisingly sexy.

"Hi," she said, her voice sounding breathy and not at all like the commanding officer who only six months ago made a jube lieutenant cry for fucking up an order so simple an untrained monkey could have completed it in its sleep.

Ollie stepped into the room. "Wow," he said, moving closer. "You look beautiful."

Mia couldn't miss the direction of his gaze. Oliver always was a boob man. "My eyes are up here, Bennett," she said, her voice regaining its usual tone of authority.

Gripping her waist in his big hands, he continued staring at her cleavage. "Yeah, but your breasts are down there, and I gotta ask, where the fuck have you been hiding those?"

The dress she'd chosen to wear wrapped around her body and overlapped in the front to create a V neckline, and the only bra she owned that went with the dress was a push-up bra that caused her very average C-cups to look more like Double-Ds.

"You know they don't look like this in real life, yeah? It's just the bra earning its hefty price-tag."

"I actually don't know that," he said, finally looking her in the eye and flashing that sexy half-grin of his. "But maybe you'll show me later?"

Mirroring his grin, she took a chance and slid her hands over his chest. *Faaark.* His body truly was solid muscle. She pressed her thighs together and tried not to squirm as an image of Ollie naked, on his knees and sexing her up flooded her mind. "It's not like you've never seen me naked before."

"True, but it's been such a long time, and my memory isn't what it used to be." He traced one finger along the edge of the V and over the curve of her breast.

The touch was so light, so intimate.

Anticipation skittered over her skin causing her to shiver, and she sucked in a shaky breath. Then she slid her hands higher, looped one around his neck, grabbed his braid. Wrapped it around her fist and pulled. Ollie's deep groan was music to her ears, and her pussy clenched in response.

"Be a good boy and maybe I'll refresh your memory," she purred, then released his hair and smoothed her hands over his shirtfront, straightened his collar. "Now, where are we going on our date. And if you say we're going to the pub, this date ends now."

"Oh, ye of little faith," he replied. "Rest assured, I have procured a private little spot where we can talk and be alone and just enjoy the evening and each other."

Narrowing her eyes, she said, "Sounds promising."

"Truly, your faith in me is overwhelming," he said drily, then took her hand in his and gave it a squeeze. "Shall we?"

Ten minutes later they were pulling into the driveway of Someday. Mia turned to Oliver from the passenger seat, confusion pinching her forehead. "A private spot, huh?"

"Best damn views in town," he replied, winking.

"And what are we supposed to eat?" The only food in the house was the tea, honey and lemons he'd left for her when he'd found her dad's flask.

"It's all taken care of, sweetling. Trust me."

Ollie hopped out of the car then ran around to the other side to help Mia out. "You okay with the stairs, or would you like me carry you?"

The work they'd done in the forge after lunch had put strain on her back and leg, but she didn't want to complain. She'd had fun helping Ollie like she used to, she just hadn't remembered it being so much hard work, or taking such a toll on her body. Still, she was hurting, and knew if she tried walking up those stairs unaided, the date would end really fast.

"Carry me, please."

"As you wish," he murmured against her lips as he swept her into his arms.

When they reached the top, he didn't put her down, but rather he followed the veranda around to the back of the house, to the place she'd stood that morning as she'd sipped her tea and contemplated her future.

But the spot was no longer empty.

An assortment of glass jars filled with flickering candles lined the space, giving it a delicate glow, and a table was set with linen, glasses and cutlery. *What the...?* Oliver put Mia back on her feet, then held out a chair for her.

Taking her seat, she said, "Ollie, when did you do all this?"

It couldn't have been in the hour between finishing

work and collecting her from her room. He might have the body of Superman but she was pretty sure he didn't have super-speed.

Looking sheepish, he took the other seat, then picked up and rang a little bell she hadn't noticed sitting on the table. "I may have had some help."

Within seconds of ringing the bell, the French doors opened and Abby and Wolf appeared, carrying two bowls of creamy pasta, a plate of thickly cut fresh bread, and an ice bucket holding a bottle of champagne.

"Wow, that's a lot of carbs," she murmured as Abby put the food on the table, then swallowed thickly as saliva filled her mouth. *Geez*, any moment now she was going to start drooling like a Saint Bernard, because wouldn't that be sexy? But the bacon carbonara smelled so fucking good.

Wolf opened the champagne and filled two glasses. "Do you require anything else?"

Ollie deferred to her. "Mia?"

Without moving her gaze from Ollie's, she shook her head. "No. I think we have everything we need." To Abby and Wolf, she added, "Thank you."

Abby laid her hand on her brother's shoulder and gave it a squeeze. "Have a good night," she said quietly, her smile filling up her face.

"See you in the morning," Wolf added with a wink, then he took Abby's hand and they disappeared around the corner of the house.

"They did all of this for us?" Mia still couldn't quite believe it.

"Jane cooked," Ollie said, "and chose the champers. But yes, they did."

Mia read the label on the bottle and her eyes shot wide. It was actual, proper French Champagne. *Fuck.* It was a fair shot better than the Passion Pop they'd shared as teenagers. Her hand shook as she reached for her glass, but before she could pick it up, Ollie took her hand in his, wrapped his thick fingers around her smaller ones.

"Is it too much?" he asked, his expression one of worry as his gaze searched hers.

Heat and moisture filled her eyes and she sniffed back the prickle of tears before they could embarrass her further. "No, it's not too much."

"Then what's wrong? Have you changed your mind? Do you want to go back to the house?"

"No, nothing like that," she hurried to assure him. "It's just that I'd forgotten." She looked around them again, took in the romantic setting of the candles and the soft evening sky and the fantastic food. The amazing company. "I'd forgotten what it's like to be home, to be surrounded by people who care." She shook her head. "I don't deserve it. Not after what I did."

Ollie's features softened and he gave her a look she hadn't seen in a long, long time. His "you're adorable but you're an idiot" look.

"Life's too short to hold grudges," he said softly. "Especially between best friends. More especially for shit we did when we were seventeen."

Mia cleared her throat in a vain attempt to dislodge the emotions choking her up. She shifted in her chair.

"Even so, I owe you an apology. I never should have left the way I did, and I'm sorry I hurt you. I never wanted that."

"I'm sorry, too."

Frowning, she said, "What do you have to be sorry for?"

"For not hopping on the next bus to Canberra and hunting your stubborn arse down."

Mia slapped her free hand over her mouth but wasn't quick enough to stop the burst of laughter from escaping her, and the tension she'd been holding on to slipped away. "I was pretty stubborn, wasn't I?"

Ollie chuckled, too. "We both were," he said, then squeezed her fingers. "I also wanted to apologise for not being here for Louisa's funeral. For not being here for you."

Mia shook her head. "It's fine, Ollie. Really."

"No, it's not fine. You needed me and I wasn't here."

"Where were you?" she asked. "I remember Abby saying you were somewhere in Europe."

"Yes, at a blacksmithing festival in the Ukraine. My sister called but I didn't get the message until it was too late. By the time I got back to Australia the funeral was over and you were gone again. I tried reaching out to you through your office, but you never replied."

"Really?"

"Really, really."

She closed her eyes and shook her head, her mouth pinched in annoyance. "Mother*fuckers*."

"What?"

Her shoulders stiffened, her eyes narrowed. "No one gave me the message," she said through gritted teeth.

Ollie shook his head. "For fuck's sake, are you kidding me?"

"I wish I was," she said, snapping open her napkin and laying it in her lap. "It was a standard tactic for the unit I was in at the time. Make me look stupid or ignorant or uncaring by not passing along pertinent information." She shook her head. "Boy club bullshit. Arseholes."

Oliver's gaze narrowed. "Are these the same arseholes who caused your habit of taking a swing at someone when you're startled?"

She pursed her lips and shook her head. "No. That trait was ingrained in me during basic training. There was this one sergeant…. He used to wake us up by grabbing our tits."

"Jesus. Mia…." Ollie looked furious.

Mia held up her hand to stop whatever heroic thing her lover was about to say next. "It's okay. I'm okay. It was a shitty lesson to learn but an important one."

But Oliver wasn't backing down. "What the fuck could you possibly learn from being sexually harassed?"

"I learned to push back, to take a stand and say no." She let her lips lift in a smirk. "I learned to use my words instead of my fists."

One blond eyebrow winged up. "Meaning?"

"Meaning guys learned very quickly not to lie about sleeping with me if they didn't want me to lie about how tiny their dicks were."

The deep rumble of Oliver's laugh coaxed out a laugh

of her own. "I'm guessing the fact you could beat the shit out of them didn't go astray either."

"Maybe," she conceded, grinning. A grin that dissolved into a sad smile as Mia recalled what they'd been talking about before getting sidetracked. "If I was still in uniform I'd certainly consider beating the shit out whomever it was that didn't pass on your message."

Ollie's smile slipped and he ducked his head, looked up at her from under his impossibly long lashes. "I had thought maybe you didn't want to talk to me, that you were mad at me for not being at the funeral."

Mia's heart broke a little at the sadness in Ollie's voice, in his eyes. "No, that wasn't it at all. I know how much you loved mum. I know you would have been there if you could. And I can't thank you enough for everything you've done since she...,"—she ducked her head and blinked away fresh tears—"you know."

Ollie lifted Mia's hand to his lips and pressed a kiss to her knuckles. "I'm sorry, Mia. I didn't mean to upset you."

That was her Ollie. Always concerned for her more than himself. "I'm all right. I just miss her."

"I miss her too," he said, giving her hand a final squeeze. "Now, eat up. Jane will have our guts for garters if we let this go cold."

They ate in companionable silence and simply enjoyed the meal and the atmosphere, and Mia did something she hadn't done on a date in a very long time.

She didn't think about work.

Instead, she shoved all thoughts of the veteran's

retreat and renovations and landscaping options and rehabilitation schedules to the back of her mind and focused on more important things, like not making a spectacle of herself by licking the bowl, because as always, Jane Melville's cooking was sublime. The pasta was so damn delicious, and—*holy shit*—French champagne was incredible.

But when the meal was done, the silence lost its companionability and took on a more nervous edge.

Did Ollie feel it too? Or was she all alone in her little bubble of anxiety and doubt?

"Would you like to dance?"

Mia fiddled with her napkin. "We don't have any music."

Ollie pulled his phone from his pocket and a few seconds later a slow jazz wafted through the space. He stood and held out his hand, pulling her to her feet when she slid her palm against his.

Staring up at her date, she wondered how they'd managed to go so long without seeing each other. It wasn't as if she'd never come home to visit her mum, but whenever she was in town, Oliver wasn't. He was always off somewhere pretending to be a Viking, or teaching people his trade.

As time wore on, the longer she went without him in her life, the more she wondered if what she'd felt for him was even real.

But now, here, dancing with Ollie, his arm around her waist, her hand held in his, her other hand resting on his powerful shoulder, and his warmth enveloping her, protecting her, she wondered how she'd ever stayed away from him.

"I wish I'd known you were coming home," Ollie said. "I would have laid out a proper welcome mat."

Mia leaned into him and rested her head on his chest, smiled when he wrapped both arms around her and kept on swaying to the music. "I didn't tell anyone I was coming home. Figured there wasn't anyone to tell. Well, besides Rafe, but I didn't want to deal with lawyers my first day back."

"And me? Why didn't you come to see me?"

She stiffened as the truth of her answer brought tears to her eyes once again. "I didn't think I'd be welcome."

"Why? Because you took my virginity then ran away and broke my heart?"

It was hard to miss the teasing tone of the question, but it still stung with a ring of truth. She nodded. "That may have had something to do with it," she whispered, unable to stop the tears slipping down her face.

"Hey. Look at me." All teasing was gone from his tone as Oliver cupped her cheeks and made her look at him, wiped away her tears and calmed her nerves with gentle strokes of his rough fingers on her face and neck. "You listen up and listen good. You will always be welcome in my life, Mia. Always."

15

Oliver stared into Mia's worried gaze and he couldn't fight it any longer. He hated seeing the constant doubt flickering over her features, so sure the hurt she'd caused him so long ago was unforgivable.

Did it still sting that she'd left him behind to chase a career? Yeah, a little bit.

Was he going to let that minor sting stop him from doing the one thing he'd wanted to do from the moment Dave had pulled back her hoodie and revealed her gorgeous face to him after so goddamn long without her?

Fuck no.

As his lips crashed against Mia's, he slid his hands down her back and tugged her closer, pulled her body into his and let her feel exactly how much he wanted her. Hell, his cock had been rock hard through most of dinner, watching the pure delight on her face as she'd enjoyed her meal. He wondered how long it had been since she'd indulged herself and eaten foods her training told her to avoid.

Too fucking long if the disappointment he'd read in her eyes when her bowl was empty was anything to go by. She wasn't in the army anymore. She didn't need to stick to such joyless restrictions. He'd feed her carbs every day if it made her happy.

"Ollie," she moaned, ripping open his shirt and attacking his neck and lower, sucking and biting a path along his collarbone until she sank her teeth into his shoulder.

Sliding his hand into her hair, he held her to him, savoured the sting of her teeth before feeling her lips and tongue as she sucked on his flesh and marked his body. Left her claim on him for everyone to see.

"Sweetling, yes."

But then she stopped and pulled away, tilted her head and furrowed her brow. Delicate fingertips traced over the tattoo on his chest. "What does it mean?"

Oliver captured her hand and brought her fingers to his lips, pressed a kiss to them, then placed her hand back on his chest. "It's the Helm of Awe, a symbol of protection."

"Protection from what?"

"Anyone who would wish me harm, either physical, spiritual... or emotional." Mia tried to pull away but he grabbed her hand and pressed it flat over the tattoo, then laid his hand on top of hers. Keeping her close. He knew what she was thinking. What was it going to take to convince her he was okay, that she'd not done anything wrong. "You didn't wish me harm, Mia."

"I may not have wished for it, but I hurt you just the same. Why aren't you more pissed off at me?"

"I told you, life's too short to hold grudges." He slid his free arm around her waist again and began swaying her in time to the music. "Would you feel better if I *was* pissed off at you?"

Mia chewed on her lip, then shook her head. "No," she grumbled.

"Would you feel better if I told you I forgive you?"

Her gaze snapped to his. "Yes," she whispered, her expression contorted with desperation. Her voice was tainted with it too and he wanted to crush it for her. The last thing she should feel with him was desperate.

"Done," he said. Over. Simple.

But Mia never could resist arguing, even when she was winning. "What do you mean 'done'? It can't be that easy."

A slow grin spread across Ollie's face as he stared down at her. "You really don't understand how this whole forgiveness thing works, do you?" He stopped swaying and cupped her cheeks. "Mia, I know why you did what you did and I forgive you for it. Fuck, I forgave you a long time ago."

"But... how? Why?"

"Louisa." The song changed and Oliver pulled Mia into another dance. "I spent a lot of time with her in the couple of years before she passed, helped her sort through the house and get it ready for you." He smiled down at her. "She told me everything, sweetling."

Mia jerked in his arms, tried to escape him again—stubborn wench—but he wouldn't let her retreat.

He wouldn't let her run away this time.

"Talk to me, Mia. Please. Let me in. You don't have to go through everything alone."

When she finally spoke, she whispered so softly he barely heard her over the music. "What did mum tell you?"

"That you were contemplating staying in Melville's Cross instead of joining up. That she feared you'd make the same mistake she made at that age and give up your dreams for a man. For me. She told me she loved your dad with all her heart, but she regretted passing up the opportunity to study piano at the Conservatorium in Sydney, that she'd diminished her own dreams to fit into your father's lifestyle. She wanted better for you, and told me she pushed you to leave earlier than you'd planned, to go while I was away for the weekend, and that's why you didn't say goodbye."

"She never told me you knew that. She only ever said you popped around for tea sometimes, to play the piano with her. Ollie, I... I don't know what to say. I was scared."

"I know."

"After we made love, it changed everything. What I thought, how I felt. I didn't know what I wanted. I questioned everything. I felt like I was letting everyone down."

"You always did put too much pressure on yourself," he scolded lightly. "I just wish you'd talked to me about it, because then I could have told you what I told Louisa. I'm a blacksmith, born and bred. I can do my job anywhere. And I've spent the last eighteen years proving that all I need is an anvil, my tool kit and a fire and I'm good to go.

"Mia, I would have followed you anywhere. Because all I wanted, all I have ever truly desired was to be with you. To be by your side." He pushed her hair away from her face, made sure she could see the sincerity in his eyes, hear it in his words. "Mia, I was in love with you." Then taking a deep breath he admitted what he'd known from the instant she'd shown up in his life again. "And sweetling, I still am."

Eyes wide and mouth hanging open, Mia just stared at him as though he'd grown a second head. But before he could even think about damage control, she blurted out, "I still love you too."

Wait. "What?"

A small laugh bubbled out of her, one that grew and grew until she was almost doubled over in riotous laughter.

Ollie wasn't sure if he should laugh too, or be offended. "What's so funny?"

"Me. You. Us. All of it. Oh my God, Ollie, we were so fucking clueless." Her shoulders continued to bounce as her laughter died down to a chuckle, and she wiped the wetness from her eyes. "Eighteen years later and not much has changed. You're still the sensitive, beautiful boy I fell for the moment we met on that stupid bus, and I'm still the same non-communicative moron I've always been."

"Moron is a bit harsh," Ollie said, grinning at Mia's outburst.

"Harsh but fair," she replied. "All my life I trained to be an officer, to make my parents proud of me. But a life in the army was never what I wanted. Not really. If I wasn't such a moron I would have told her that. Honestly, why the fuck did you ever put up with me? I had to have been the most boring kid in school. Always making sure I said the right things and did the right things and got the best grades. Always, always towing the line and never really living for myself."

"Not always. There was that one time you almost got expelled for beating the shit out of three guys."

"They deserved it," she spat, her expression fierce. "They were hurting you."

"Until you rescued me." He stroked her cheek. "Always my protector."

"And you were always mine." She leaned into his touch, turned her head to press a kiss to his palm, then whispered, "This is crazy though, right?"

Staring up at him again, her expression was part manic, part awe, as though she wasn't really sure what they were doing or how they got there.

He knew the feeling.

"We're crazy," she said, continuing her train of thought. "How can we possibly feel this way? We haven't seen in each other in a lifetime. How do we know what we're feeling isn't just, I don't know, nostalgia?"

Ollie stared at her lips once more, ached for another taste. "We don't," he said, grinning again. "And we won't until we try." He traced his fingertips along the neckline of her dress, savoured the heat of her skin, the soft curve of her breast. "You do want to try, don't you, sweetling?"

As Mia nodded, her expression smoothed out, grew less confused and more carnal. Sliding her hands over his chest again, she pushed his shirt off his shoulders and pinched her bottom lip between her teeth. "Yes, I want that very much."

"Good."

Before she could change her mind, Oliver swept Mia into his arms and crashed his lips against hers. It was the work of a moment to strip her out of her dress and bra and wrap her legs around his waist.

"Ollie," she moaned against his mouth, raking her nails down his biceps, leaving a stinging trail in her wake.

He loved it.

He craved it.

Wanted more of it.

"Mia, tell me what you want. Tell me what you need."

Her hooded gaze met his and his cock hammered at his zipper, desperate for release. Mia was born to command him. "I want you on your knees and your tongue in my cunt," she growled, then licked a path up the length of his neck until she reached his ear and bit down hard. "I want to come all over your face," she purred, "and then all over your cock."

She pulled back and stared at him and Ollie almost swallowed his own damn tongue at the look on her face. He'd seen that look before, a long time ago.

Major Mia had come out to play.

And she liked to play rough.

"You should probably hold on to something," he said.

Mia wrapped her arms around his neck and he gripped her arse in one hand and swept clean the table with the other. Bowls and glassware and cutlery crashed to the floor. The ice bucket fell and the bottle of champagne tipped over, the last of its contents splashing against the timber decking, but Ollie didn't care.

As soon as Mia's backside hit the table, he hit the floor, going to his knees before her as she'd commanded.

Slowly, he slid his palms from her knees to her inner thighs, taking his time to both savour her body and tease it. She'd always liked the feel of his hands on her body, even before they'd crossed that line from friendship to... more. She liked the roughness of his skin, and the heat. Liked how his palms lightly scratched her.

He followed the path of his hand with his lips, leaving wet kisses on her supple flesh, teasing her with tiny nips of his teeth and enjoying the tiny sounds of pleasure she made in response.

Mia wasn't the only one who liked to bite.

When he reached her centre, he pressed his face against the soft lace of her panties and breathed her in, nuzzled into the softness of her core and drew her scent inside himself. Then he pinched the garment between his teeth and slowly dragged them off her.

Above him he heard Mia's breathing hitch. She may have been in control, but that didn't mean he wasn't going to stretch this out. He wanted to make it good for her, wanted to give her what she craved but with a little Ollie flair.

Reaching back for his braid, he unfastened the tie in the end of it and let his hair flow free. Dragged it lightly over her thighs, tickling her until she said, "I gave you an order, Bennett."

Ollie grinned at Mia's breathless demand. He loved knowing she was as worked up as him as he unzipped his jeans and freed his aching dick. "As you wish," he whispered against her pussy, then licked along her slit in one long sweep of his tongue.

The instant he pulled away, Mia's hips bucked up searching for more. Ollie gripped her thighs and pushed them down and wide, held her captive to her need. "I know you want to come, Mia, but you have to let me do this my way. You have to surrender some of that control. You have to trust me, sweetling."

Her body fell very still but he could hear her ragged breathing. "I do trust you, baby," she said quietly, reaching for him.

Resting his chin on her mound, he stared along the length of her body, all laid out like a feast for one, and let her fist her hands in his hair again, let her direct him where she needed him most. But once he was in position, he took back control.

Ollie flicked the tip of his tongue over and around Mia's clit, teased the sensitive little nub over and over as she writhed beneath him.

"Oh fuck! Ollie... more!"

He gave her more. He gave her so much more. As he laved her clit with his tongue, he also slid two fingers deep inside her, pistoned them in and out with increasing speed as he licked her clit with more forceful strokes of his tongue.

Mia's hands tightened in his hair, tugged and released and pulled again. A sure sign she was fighting off her oncoming wave of pleasure, trying to prolong it, control it.

But Ollie wanted her to lose control.

He wanted Major Mia to let go of all the fear and the anger and the pain she held inside her, all the shit she kept to herself because she didn't trust anyone to stand by her side and help her carry that load.

She'd always been too hard on herself. Had always put everyone else first. But she would learn. He would teach her, show her.

Mia wasn't going anywhere without him ever again.

He would help her, protect her. He would put her first and treat her with the respect she deserved. He would love her with everything he had to give.

When her orgasm hit, her thighs twitched and her hips bucked and Ollie sucked her clit until she was screaming his name and clawing at his shoulders, demanding he fuck her.

Ridding himself of the last of his clothes, Oliver

rolled on a condom and lined his body up with hers, but before he pushed inside, he took her hands and pulled her to him.

"I don't want you to hurt your back," he murmured against her lips. Then he sat his arse down on a dining chair and helped Mia straddle him. Groaned as she sank down on his rock hard erection and their bodies became one.

No more words passed between them.

None were needed.

Ollie cupped Mia's arse in his big hands and gently squeezed the firm globes as he rocked her body against his. The languorous glide of her tight pussy squeezing his cock over and over was as near to heaven as he'd been in the longest time.

Mia leaned forwards and attacked his neck, nipped at him and licked him, sucked his flesh and marked him again. And when she slid her hands through his long hair, stroked it, played with it, tucked a lock of it under her nose like a moustache and made him laugh, he knew what he felt for her was real.

He couldn't remember another woman who turned him on and made him laugh so much at the same time. That heart he'd given her all those years ago, that soul, they still belonged to her.

As he watched her eyes close and her mouth open on a gasp, he stole a kiss from her. A kiss she deepened as her body clenched down on his and shook with the force of her second release, causing his to quickly follow.

Tearing her mouth away from his she cried his name

as he shouted hers, then he wrapped his arms around her and held her tight. Exalted in the feel of her sweaty body stuck to his as their breathing calmed and their heartbeats slowed to normal.

Normal.

Oliver let himself chuckle at the notion.

Where he and Emilia Caldwell were concerned, nothing would ever be normal again.

16

The next morning, Mia woke up in Oliver's bed.

And found his side of it empty.

Turning to look at the ancient clock radio she couldn't believe he still had, or that still worked, she saw it was only five-thirty. So where the bloody hell was he?

Her best friend turned lover?

Slipping from the bed, she grabbed Oliver's shirt and pulled it on, then left to use the toilet. On her way back to bed she heard voices coming from the kitchen. Following the sound, she found Ollie and his sister sitting at the big wooden kitchen table, drinking tea and passing a notepad back and forth.

When she entered the room, they both looked up and smiled, happy to see her. Her heart swelled at the simple, familial gesture and she knew she would never regret the decisions that had brought her back here. "Good morning," she said quietly.

"We didn't wake you, did we, sweetling?"

"Nah. Army brat, remember? I've been getting up before the crack of dawn since I was a kid."

Ollie shifted in his chair and offered his lap as a seating option. Which Mia readily accepted.

And why wouldn't she? The man was sex on a stick and he was all hers. He wasn't wearing his usual uniform of jeans and a T-shirt though, and Mia marvelled at how much longer his legs looked in boardshorts.

She also appreciated the fact he wasn't wearing a shirt.

Seeing all that naked muscle on display just did things to her. Not that his jeans and T-shirts did such a great job of disguising it for anything other than what it was. And when the hell did he get so jacked anyway? Mia had never wanted to be a punny slogan T-shirt so much in her life, simply so she could lovingly hug and caress his biceps all damn day, stroke his abs. Soak up his heady masculine scent.

Great. Now she was horny again. And judging by the look on Ollie's face as he watched her approach, and the slight flex of his biceps, he knew exactly where her mind was at. Hell, it was the same place it was at for most of the previous night.

In his pants.

Oliver Bennett had only gotten better with age. Even the man-bun was beginning to grow on her. And as for the beard...? If she'd known how utterly amazing it felt when a bearded bloke went down on her, she might have made more of an effort to eat avocado and date hipsters.

As Mia curled her long frame up in Ollie's lap, she rested her head on his shoulder and traced her fingertip over the runic tattoo that snaked around his forearm. When she'd asked him about it the previous night, he'd told her each set of runes spelled out the names of his family. Then he'd pointed out a set of three symbols in a contrasting blue ink.

"And this is you. This is Mia."

"I thought you said these were the names of your family?"

He'd sighed then kissed her. "What's it going to take for you to understand? You *are* my family."

Now as she sat quietly in his lap, listening to him chat with his sister as he rubbed circles against her lower back, soothing the mild ache she still held there from the night before, she was beginning to understand.

Oliver Bennett had been looking out for her from the moment she'd met him on the school bus when they were twelve. He'd tried to protect her by pushing her away but she'd forced her way inside his bubble and set up camp. Five years later she'd pushed him away, too scared of her own feelings to even let him anywhere near her bubble.

But when she needed him, he was there. No questions asked. No grudges held.

He loved her.

Like family.

"What are you two doing?" she asked, groaning when Ollie rubbed a particularly sore spot.

"Sorry, sweetling," he whispered.

"We're working out our overlap for the week," Abby replied, getting to her feet. "You want a cuppa?"

"Sure, but what do mean by overlap?"

"When the forge was built it was mostly used for making horseshoes and tools. It was never designed for things as big as those driveway gates I'm making," Ollie explained, "so Abbs and I have to schedule when we make certain items so we know we'll have enough room to move."

"You need your own forge," his sister said from the other side of the kitchen.

"Now there's an idea." Ollie sipped his tea, then shook his head. "But where would I put it, eh?"

Mia stiffened as an idea struck her, an idea so pure and simple and right that it was out of her mouth before she could overthink it. "Someday."

"What?"

"There's plenty of room at Someday. You could build your own forge there." When Ollie didn't answer, she ducked her head and half-shrugged. "If you wanted to."

A grinned curled his mouth and her heart skipped a beat at the sight, especially when he set his tea aside and wrapped both arms around her waist, nuzzled against her throat. "Emilia Caldwell, are you asking me to move in with you?"

She blinked as she wondered the same thing. "I suppose I am," she said slowly before nodding. "Yes, I'm asking you to move in with me."

"Who's moving where?" Wolf asked, yawning as he shuffled into the kitchen. He moved straight to Abby and pressed a kiss to her forehead. *"Guten morgen, liebchen."*

"I'm moving into Mia's house," Ollie announced, then he stood, taking her with him and tossed her over his shoulder.

"What are you doing?" Mia squealed.

"Celebrating," he said, and slapped her arse.

"Hey!"

"She'll take a raincheck on the tea, thanks Abbs. See ya'."

"Oliver Ulysses Bennett, you put me down right now."

"Nope. And I'd stop wriggling if I were you. That's a long way down."

"Put me down or I will bite you."

Ollie laughed and slid his free hand between her thighs. "Try it and see what happens."

So she did. She tried it. Just as Ollie kicked open the door to his bedroom, she yanked down the top of his boardshorts and bit him. Right where his waist met the top curve of his perfect arse.

His manly yelp made her laugh. His unceremonious dumping of her in the middle of his bed made her vow retribution. At least it would have, had he not immediately kicked the door closed again, dropped down on top of her and ripped open the shirt she was wearing. The act was so violent, so primal, and made her heart race.

Then he pinned her down and stole her breath away with his kiss. A slow, sensuous kiss that made her toes curl and her pussy clench with need.

And when he worked his way over her jaw and down her neck, along her collarbone and over her breast, she was unashamedly squirming, craving his next touch, his next kiss or lick or bite.

"Sweetling," Ollie breathed, blowing cool air across her nipples, causing them to tighten into hard little peaks then sinking his teeth into them, tugging on them, making her cry out for more.

"Ollie, please." Mia wrestled free of his grip and tightened her hands in the loose strands of his long hair, then thrust her chest towards him, forcing more of her breast into his mouth.

He grunted at the movement but took the hint and showered her breasts with so much attention that when he blew across her nipples again, she almost leapt off the bed, the ecstasy of it all almost more than she could bare.

"You're pampering me," she whispered when he started kissing a trail between her breasts and over her stomach.

He lifted his gaze to hers and she drowned in the lust she saw there, dark and heated and necessary. She hoped he saw in her eyes how much she wanted him too. How much she craved him. "Anything for my queen," he breathed, then lowered his mouth and licked her cunt like it was his most favourite thing to do.

There was no other way to describe Oliver's level of enthusiasm for the act.

He was a pussy eating god.

And it didn't take long to make her scream his name.

17

Ollie awoke with a jolt. Someone was banging on his bedroom door.

"Ollie? Did you hear me? They're here."

Mia shifted beside him, wrapped her arm tighter around him and snuggled down in the bedding. He gave her a shake. "Wake up, love. We have guests."

Her only response was to groan and burrow deeper into his side. "It's Sunday. It's sleep-in day."

"What happened to 'I'm an army brat, I like getting up at dawn'?"

"I never said I liked it," she grumbled. "Besides, you wore me out again with all the pussy eating and the orgasms."

"And you wore me out with that thing you did that I cannot wait for you to do again, but sweetling, we have visitors. We have to get up."

"Do we have to wear pants?"

"Unless you want to explain to Charlie why you're not wearing pants, then yes, you have to wear pants."

"Ugh. Charlie? Why?"

"Did I mention that Charlie is an architect who specialises in renovating and modernising old Queenslanders?"

Mia threw him a dirty look. "Must have slipped your mind."

They climbed out of the bed and found enough clothing to cover themselves. Mia for the quick trip to the room next door, Ollie for the bathroom.

Grabbing her hand, he tugged her closer. "He's not as annoying as he used to be," he said, placing a quick kiss on her forehead. "I promise."

But she didn't look convinced as she slipped out of his room and disappeared. And just in time too, because two gangly teenage girls came bursting through his door and tackled him to the bed.

"Uncle Ollie!"

"Good morning, miladies. I didn't know you two were coming up today." If he had, he would have locked his door and swept the room to make sure it was PG13 before allowing them access. As it was he was pretty sure there was nothing of an overtly adult nature lying about.

"Dad promised to take us out for milkshakes," Josie said.

"And we wanted to see if Jane had exploded yet," Diana, the more morbid of the two girls, added as she mimed an alien bursting from her stomach.

Next to appear in his doorway was their father, his

brother, Charlie. "Why are you still in bed, man? Late night?"

"Something like that." Then he raised his eyebrows at his brother in a suggestive manner, silently pleading with him for help.

Charlie grinned and Ollie knew he'd be paying for it later. "All right, girls. Give your poor ol' uncle Ollie some space so he can have a shower and get dressed."

The twins start complaining, until their father threatened to cancel their milkshake date. "Fine," they conceded together, then left with Charlie.

On his way to the bathroom, Ollie knocked on Mia's door, but she didn't answer.

Because she was already in the bathroom, standing in the shower, about to turn it on.

"Are you trying to give me a heart attack?" she snapped, one arm wrapped around her breasts and her opposite hand shielding her pussy from view.

Ollie's cock hardened so fucking fast at the sight of her, he nearly lost his balance from the loss of blood to his brain. "You didn't lock the door."

"Shit. I thought I did. Sorry," she said, lowering her arms and giving him a full frontal view of the sexiest woman he'd ever seen.

He made a show of locking the door, then kicked off his pants and fisted his hand around his cock. "Mind of I join you?"

Mia's gaze had dropped to his thick cock and the way he slid his hand along its length. Ollie adored watching her eyes glaze over with lust, loved how the bright blue colour would darken and grow stormy. She didn't answer, only nodded.

Stepping into the shower behind her, they waited for the water to reach temperature. "I'd hoped I wouldn't have to shower this morning. Not after I spent so much time between your pretty thighs."

Mia frowned at him, his meaning totally lost on her. "What?"

"My beard, sweetling. I was looking forward to carrying the scent of your sweet cunt around with me all day. But my nieces are here, so...."

"So you'll just have to lick my pussy again later, after they leave," she said, walking her fingers down his chest.

"I like the way you think. But what are we going to do about this?" Anchoring his hands on his hips, he stared at his dick. "I can't go out there looking like this."

"Well, I suppose we could have sex again," she suggested, sounding magnanimous, even as the lines around her mouth told him she was trying desperately not to laugh.

But Ollie shook his head. "I didn't bring a condom with me."

Mia shrugged. "I'm on birth control."

"Pregnancy isn't the only thing you can catch, Mia," he said drily.

"I wouldn't have suggested it if I wasn't 100 percent sure I was good to go. Unless... are you...?"

"What? No. I'm clean, I just... I've never had sex without protection before."

The knowledge seemed to shock her. "Really?"

It shouldn't have. Not with his parentage. "Really, really."

Mia dragged him farther under the water and slid her arms around his waist. "We don't have to do anything you don't want to do," she assured him quietly. "And it just so happens I know a lot of ways we can take care of your problem that don't involve my pussy."

Ollie grinned at Mia as she lowered herself to her knees. "You do, do you?"

"Uh-huh." And that was all she said before guiding his cock between her lips and sucking him down her throat.

It took everything in Ollie, every scrap of willpower he owned not to call out her name, or even groan too loudly in case they were found out. Sliding his fingers into her hair and cupping the back of her head in one hand, he leaned against the shower wall with the other. Held them both up.

Mia's technique was sublime.

The way she used her teeth to tease his shaft, her tongue to lick in long soothing strokes. Her lips to pull him back in after letting him slip out. And then she cupped his balls and gently kneaded and tugged.

He thought his head might explode from the pleasure before the rest of him did.

"Oh, fuck. Mia. Sweetling. I'm gunna come, baby. I'm gunna come. Shit."

Ollie's body stiffened and jerked as he shot his load down Mia's throat. His hand tightened in her hair as he held her to him, the wet strands tangling around his fist, twisting around his fingers.

When his orgasm finally subsided and his body stopped shaking, he helped her to her feet and wrapped her in his arms. "I guess we should have that shower now," he murmured against her hair, then pulled back to stare down at her. "Would you like me to wash you?" he asked, his tongue slipping along his lower lip as his fingertips caressed the underside of her breasts.

Mia snorted and slapped his hands away. "You do that and we're never leaving this bathroom."

18

After they finished their dirty shower and got dressed, Ollie took Mia to the lounge room to meet the members of the Bennett family she didn't already know, and get reacquainted with the ones she did.

"This is Lucy," Oliver said, introducing the blonde sitting on a cushion on the floor by Toby's feet.

The woman had severe burn scars on the right side of her face and neck, but her intelligent gaze and bright smile went a long way to disarming any unease Mia might have otherwise felt at the sight of the ruined flesh. And it was hard to tell with her curled up on the floor, but Lucy looked to be of a similar height and size as Mia. She wore a simple silver chain around her neck with a heart-shaped pendant on it, and an engagement ring on her left hand.

The woman was obviously Toby's submissive, but judging by the way he was lovingly stroking her hair and staring at her as though she'd hung the stars in the sky, Lucy had the giant man wrapped completely around her little finger.

They were getting married the following weekend, and Toby had asked if he could use the gardenia blooms from her mother's garden in the bouquets. Gardenias were Lucy's favourite and Someday had an overabundance of them on the property.

They also invited her to the wedding, insisted on it, in fact. She didn't miss the smug "I told you so" grin Oliver threw at her when she accepted the invitation, and maybe—*maybe*—he was right. Maybe her fear of being unwelcome was all in her head. But then, the Bennetts had always accepted her without question. Had always made her feel like one of their own.

Even Charlie.

Who was still a smart-arse, by the way, but at least he'd lost his immature edge. Perhaps fatherhood had done that to him, mellowed him somewhat, because his daughters were absolutely lovely, and Mia could hardly believe they were only just turning fourteen.

"Are you sure they're yours?" she teased.

"Fuck off, Caldwell."

"Actually, Charlie, Mia could use your advice." She shot daggers at Ollie for bringing up the house but he didn't seem to care. As he proved when he continued, "She wants to turn Someday into a veteran's retreat, but the old house needs a lot of work. Do you reckon you could take a look while you're here?"

To Mia's surprise, he said, "Sure. I'll pop over after I take the girls out for milkshakes."

"You will?" she said, still a little confused by how easy that had been. How Charlie hadn't insisted on something embarrassing as recompense for his time and effort.

"Yeah. Happy to, if you that's what you want."

"Um, okay," she said, a tiny frown pinching her brows together, her brain still not quite willing to believe him. "Thanks."

"A veteran's retreat is an interesting idea," Lucy said. "Do you know what sort of activities you want to offer yet?"

"I want to take advantage of some of the lesser known tourist traps, like the rainforest walks and trips to some of the smaller beaches along the coast, but also offer all the usual stuff too. Camping, day-trips to the waterfalls, rock-climbing—"

"Lucy's a rock climber," one of the twins said.

"Really? Where do you climb?"

"The last few years I've been a gym climber only, but *someone*,"—she poked Toby's knee—"won't even let me do that anymore."

Toby made a growling sound. "Baby, you're pregnant."

"Barely," Lucy grumbled.

"Do we really need to have this conversation again?"

Lucy pursed her lips then shook her head. "No, Master."

"Good, then stop sulking. It doesn't become you," Toby said, his deep voice vibrating with command.

"Yeah well I'd say being a bossy prick doesn't become you, either," Lucy said, "but you know I'd be lying."

"Cheeky." Toby chuckled and bent his head down to kiss her in what could have easily turned into an x-rated display of public affection, had it not been for the teenage girls making gagging noises.

"Eww," the twins complained. "Dad, they're kissing again."

Oliver slung his arms around their shoulders. "You won't mind so much one day, my loves."

Both girls turned to him and scoffed. "*Yeeeah*, we'll stick with milkshakes thanks."

"Thank God," Charlie muttered under his breath, then added, "Speaking of which, are you two ready to go?"

"While they're doing that," Lucy said, "could we look at Someday? I'd like to see these million dollar views for myself, if that's okay?"

"Absolutely," Mia said. "We can head over now if you like. Toby can check out the garden, I'll show you the views and Charlie can meet us there later. And hey, if you like what you see, we could arrange to have some of your wedding photos taken there too."

Ollie took Mia's hand and smiled at her, his smug grin replaced by an expression of what looked suspiciously like contentment. She felt it too, the ease of which she'd slipped back into this life she'd left behind, as though she'd never left in the first place.

When they arrived at Someday, Toby and Ollie headed straight around to the back of the house to where the bulk of the gardenia bushes grew, while she pointed out to Lucy some of the improvements she wanted to make. Like the possibility of lowering the house and adding the accessibility ramp.

"And will the retreat just be for veterans?" Lucy asked.

Mia rubbed her leg as she got out of the car. Going down on Ollie in the shower had aggravated something and the dull ache that came and went was back again. Oliver had noticed her limping before they'd left the house and insisted she take her walking stick.

"That was the plan, why?"

"I come from a family of firefighters. I was just thinking it would be awesome for emergency services personnel too."

"That's not a bad idea, actually," Mia said, nodding. "Definitely something to think about, anyway. I do know one thing though, I don't want to turn the place into one of those corporate retreats full of CEO douchebags, you know?"

"I hear that," Lucy agreed with a snort of laughter, then shaded her eyes with her hand and looked towards the road. "Who's that?"

Mia turned in time to see Greg Wheeler hop out of his car and stroll up her driveway, looking even more smug than he had the day before. She didn't have time for this man or his mission, and she wasn't beating around the bush about it anymore.

"Oh for fuck's sake. Why are you here, Mr Wheeler? I've already told you I'm not interested in selling my house. Please leave."

But the smarmy prick didn't give up. "You will sell to me, Miss Caldwell, and I'm going to tell you why," he said with a broad smile that reminded Mia of a demented clown.

"Oh my God," she groaned in an exaggerated display of boredom. "I couldn't give two shits why you think I should sell you my home. And how the fuck do you know my name? No. You know what? I don't care."

Turning her back on him, Mia moved towards the stairs, hoping the patronising fuck-knuckle in the suit would take the hint and bugger off before he saw her struggle to climb the damn things.

She should be so lucky.

"I know a lot of things about you, Mia."

Hearing this cretin say her name made her skin crawl. "Like what?"

"Like you'll never be able to look after a property of this size on a military pension. And certainly not with your limited physical capabilities," he said, his voice dripping with fake concern as he gestured to her walking stick. "Selling to me is the only smart option. Be smart, Mia."

She laughed low and slow and shook her head. *Is this idiot for real?* She held up her walking stick, making a show of its beautiful brass handle. "Tell me, Mr Wheeler, do you know why my walking stick has this shiny metal knob on the end of it?"

The man frowned at her like she was nuts. "What does tha—"

"It's so you don't get an infection when I shove it up your arse," Mia snarled, cutting him off like a pro. Lord knew she'd had enough men demonstrate the action to her over the years. Beside her, Lucy snorted and held up her fist. Mia bumped it.

"Now listen here—"

"No. You listen. From the moment you walked onto *my* property, you have questioned my integrity, my capabilities, and my intelligence, so let me make myself crystal clear. I am *never* selling you my house. Never. So why don't you get back in your clown car and fuck the hell off before I'm forced to buy a new walking stick."

The realtor flicked his gaze from Mia to Lucy, outright shock painted across his overly tanned face. If he was looking for a softer target, he wouldn't find one. Lucy folded her arms over her chest. "Don't look at me, mate. I'm an ex-fiery. You wanna see what I can do with an axe?"

When the idiot still didn't make a move to leave—obviously too shocked to put one foot in front of the other after being threatened by not one but two women who were over his shit—Mia strode towards him and made him move. He practically ran back to his car and sped off down the street.

When she turned back to the house, however, she realised it wasn't her he'd run from. Toby and Oliver Bennett, two of the biggest men in the country, stood with their arms folded over their chests and scowls etched so deeply into their expressions, Mia feared they'd never get them out.

"You okay, love?" Ollie.

"Baby, you good?" Toby.

When both women assured the brothers they were fine, the men vanished back into the garden.

"What an arsehole," Lucy muttered. "You should report this to Scott. Just in case."

Mia frowned. "Just in case of what?"

"Just in case of whatever. You never know what these crazies are capable of until it's too late. Like the woman who tried to hurt Jane last year. That was a mess and a half."

"Someone tried to hurt Jane? What the hell happened?"

Lucy filled her in about the graffiti and the fire and the car crash and by the time she was finished, Mia had her phone in her hand and the number for the Melville's Cross Police station on the screen. "You're right. I'll give the good sergeant a call."

"While you do that, I'll make us a cuppa," Lucy said, then took the front steps two at a time.

Mia watched her new friend with an envious eye. For a woman who was five years older than Mia, and almost two months pregnant, Lucy Barton was insanely fit, and for a teeny-tiny moment, Mia's insecurities joined forces with the echoes of the shithead realtor's words about her limited capabilities, making her feel like an inferior woman.

"I hate you," she muttered, watching the other

woman disappear into the house, knowing the words were a complete lie.

Lucy was awesome, and Mia couldn't hate her if she tried. Besides, it wasn't Lucy's fault Mia couldn't run up flights of stairs anymore.

That was all on her and her choice of career.

After calling the police station and leaving a brief message with the constable, Mia slowly made her way upstairs to her waiting cup of tea and the sense of serenity that came with it.

"How do you like your tea?" Lucy asked as Mia entered the kitchen.

"Black, please," she said and fetched the leftover honey and lemons Ollie had left for her on Friday night.

Tea in hand, Mia showed Lucy to the back veranda and the magnificent view beyond it, but Lucy seemed more interested in other things. "So what's the deal with you and Oliver?" she said.

Mia stilled. "What deal?"

"Oh come on. You two haven't seen each other for two decades and now you're moving in together? Is the sex really that good?"

Her serenity blown to shit, Mia stared at Lucy with wide eyes. She had no response. What the hell *could* she say? "Why yes, actually, Oliver's cock is perfect, not only in size and style, but it's attached to a man who actually knows how to use it. Huzzah!"

Taking pity on her, Lucy explained, "Look, I adore Abby, but she's my future sister-in-law, and I could *really* use a girlfriend I can talk to about the size of Toby's dick."

Turning her head just in time to send it over the railing instead of directly into Lucy's face, hot tea sprayed from Mia's mouth. After taking a moment to regain her composure, she stared at her new friend with her mouth gaping open before bursting out laughing.

"Oh my God, I did not need that image in my head," she laughed, then narrowed her gaze. "But out of curiosity…," she said, dropping her voice to a whisper as if afraid the man in question would overhear, "how big are we talking?"

Lucy grinned and held her hands an unfathomable width apart. Was she measuring a penis or a prize winning cucumber?

"No way." Mia shook her head, her eyes impossibly wide. "That can't be right. That's inhuman."

"Oh, you have no idea," Lucy said, sighing. "I can't wait to marry that man."

"One more week and the wait is over," Mia said. "And yes, the sex really is that good. Also, I'm never looking Toby in the eyes again."

19

On Monday morning it was decided that Oliver should have Rafe's spare set of keys for Someday, and by lunchtime, he was strolling through the door of Rafe's legal office to pick them up.

"Hey, Sue," Ollie said to the receptionist. "I'm here to pick up some keys from Rafe. They're the ones we had cut for the Caldwell house a few months back."

Rafe's usually unflappable receptionist stared at Ollie like she'd seen a ghost, then buzzed his brother.

Rafe appeared a moment later but not from his office. He came from the direction of the conference room. "Ollie, come with me. Now."

"Hey, it's cool. If you're busy I can come back later."

His older brother frowned at him then pointed to his office. "Now."

Once inside his office, Rafe shut the door and told Oliver to sit down.

"I'm good," Ollie replied, confusion causing his brow to furrow. "What's going on?"

Rafe sat down behind his desk but continued staring at Oliver in that peevish manner he had when things were not going the way he wanted. "Do you know a woman named Ella Mulligan?"

The name brought an instant smile to his face. "Yeah, of course. She's a Viking re-enactor like me. I used to see her around all the time when I was on the festival circuit. Not so much these days, but yeah, she's a mate."

"When was the last time you saw her?"

Ollie didn't even need to think about it. He saw Ella the same time every year. "July last year, at the Abbey Medieval Festival." But then a bad feeling gripped his chest and he felt a powerful need to breathe deeply and calm his pulse. "Why the questions, Raffy. What's going on?"

"Did you ever have sex with Miss Mulligan?"

"What the—"

"Answer the question, Oliver." Rafe was in full lawyer mode now. No room for error, no time for jokes.

"Yes. Once. But it was years ago. She'd just been through a bad break-up and we'd both had too much mead. One thing led to another...."

Rafe watched Ollie like a hawk and he knew what his brother was looking for. Ollie wasn't the only one who knew how to read people, and Rafe was looking for a lie. "Did you use protection?"

"Okay, now you're just being offensive. Of course I used protection. I've never been *that* drunk."

"Okay." Rafe rubbed at his forehead like he did when he had a headache. "Good."

Oliver rested his hands on the edge of his brother's desk and leaned forwards. "Rafe, what's going on? Why all the questions? Is Ella okay?"

"Sit down, Ollie. Please."

His brother's hollow tone had Ollie sinking into a chair without argument. "What is it? What's wrong?"

"I'm sorry to tell you this, but Miss Ella Mulligan was killed—"

"What? No!"

"I'm so sorry, Ollie. It was a car crash. Two weeks ago. A drunk ran a red light and ploughed into her car on her way home from work. She was killed instantly."

Oliver stared unseeingly at the wall behind his brother's head. A woman was dead. A kind woman, a fun woman. His friend.

"Ollie, there's more."

Jumping to his feet, he made a beeline for the door. "No. No more. I've heard enough." But before he could escape the suffocating confines of the office, his brother said something that stopped him cold.

"She had a daughter, Ollie. A daughter her parents claim is yours."

Slowly, Oliver turned around and faced Rafe. "You wanna say that again?"

"The people in my conference room are Ella's parents. They've been trying to find you since she died, to convince you to take your daughter, to accept your responsibility and raise the child." He sighed and rubbed his forehead again. "Ella's father is unwell. Her mother has been doing her best to look after her husband and the child full-time but she's not coping."

Ollie shook his head. "This is a joke, right? Some sick joke of Charlie's? You're lying, right?"

"I would never lie to you, Oliver. Not about something like this, and you know that."

"No." He shook his head, denial thick in his veins. "They must have me confused with someone else. I saw Ella six months ago. As far as I knew, she didn't have any kids. None she ever told me about, anyway. Certainly none she claimed were mine. If we had a daughter together, why didn't she tell me?" He rubbed at the dull ache in his chest, muttered, "We used protection."

"No contraception is foolproof, Ollie. I know that better than anyone. And I've seen the birth certificate. It's legitimate. Oliver Ulysses Bennett is listed as the girl's father."

Ollie flopped back into the chair. "Well... shit."

"Yeah. Shit."

Panic warred with a sudden excitement that bubbled up inside him and made him grip the arms of the chair so tightly his knuckles blanched. This feeling, it felt a lot like fear. "What do I do?"

"What do you want to do?"

He didn't even have to think about it. "If I have a daughter out there, I want her. I won't abandon my child the way my mother abandoned me."

Rafe nodded. "I thought you might say that. Come with me and you can meet Ella's parents."

"And the girl? Jesus, I don't even know her name."

"Her name is Sigrid," Rafe said. "Sigrid Olivia Bennett."

"Sigrid," he repeated, smiling. "It's old Norse. It means victory. And Olivia...." Ella had remembered his story about the Bennett family tradition. "Is she here? Can I meet her?" His heart beat at a mile a minute at the thought. What would she look like? Sound like?

What was he going to tell Mia?

"No, she's in daycare today, but we can discuss that later. Right now we need to get some other things sorted out. Come on."

Once introductions were made and everyone was seated, Ollie took the time to study the couple sitting opposite him. He could see the resemblance between Ella and the two strangers before him, and wondered again what Sigrid looked like. Would she favour her mother's looks or his?

Mr Mulligan folded his arms over his chest and sniffed, his disdain for Ollie as clear as the nose on his face. "So you're Siggy's deadbeat dad." He sniffed again. "I'm not impressed."

"I beg your pardon?" Ollie's temper flared. "How dare you accuse me—"

"Ollie." Rafe gripped his shoulder. "Let me do the talking."

"Mr Mulligan, as I expressed to you before, my brother was unaware of his daughter's existence. If, indeed, she even is his daughter."

"What are saying?"

Ollie had to agree with the older man. "Yeah, what are you saying?"

"The fact of the matter is that Ella lied to you all. She lied about Oliver to both of you," he said, indicating her parents. "And she lied by omission by not telling you about Sigrid," he said to Oliver. "How do we know she didn't also lie about who her daughter's father is? Maybe the reason she didn't tell Oliver about her is because he isn't actually her father."

Ella's dad slammed his fist on the table. "Are you calling my daughter a whore?"

"Not at all," Rafe said, his composure unwavering. "But by your own earlier admission, and Oliver's confirmation, Ella was in a relationship just prior to the time she spent with him. It's possible this other man is Sigrid's father but she used Oliver's name on the birth certificate because they were friends."

"But it's also possible that Oliver is Siggy's father, isn't it?" Mrs Mulligan asked, a nervous edge in her voice.

Rafe nodded. "Yes, it is. Which is why I propose we conduct a paternity test to be sure."

"And what'll that cost me?" Mulligan grumbled.

"Nothing," Oliver said. "I'll pay for it."

Mulligan's dismissive gaze flicked over Ollie again, probably noting the black soot under his fingernails and the sweat lining his face. "You sure you can afford it?"

Now it was Ollie's turn to scoff. He might not have been as wealthy as some of his siblings, but he did all right for himself. "It's not a problem."

After the Mulligans agreed to the paternity test, they readied to leave.

"How long until we know the results?" Mrs Mulligan asked as she dug through her handbag.

"It usually only takes a week or so," Rafe said, "but I know you have other concerns so I will ask them to put a rush on it."

"Thank you," she said. "I appreciate that." And then she handed Ollie a photograph. "This is a picture I took of Sigrid just before Christmas. She'll be three in April."

Oliver took the photo and stared at it. The little girl was sitting on a merry-go-round and waving at her grandmother as she took the picture. She had blonde curly hair like her mother's, but her bright blue eyes were a mirror for his. And that's when it hit, a feeling of utter wretchedness that he'd let her down. He'd left his daughter unprotected and alone.

His chest tightened and his tears fell. "She's beautiful."

A cool, gentle hand cupped his cheek and Mrs Mulligan's voice was filled with sympathy, with pity. "You really didn't know, did you?"

He shook his head. "Why didn't she tell me?"

"Ella had her own way of doing things. She could be stubborn, and never knew when to ask for help, but she was a good mother. She loved that little girl with all her heart."

And I will too.

"What happens if he's not the father?" Mulligan

asked Rafe, and Ollie wanted to punch him for even thinking it.

"If the test is negative and Oliver is not the father, then there's little else we can do for you outside of putting you in touch with child protection services. They should be able to help you locate Ella's ex, but they won't force him to take a paternity test. He would need to volunteer."

"Then I'll pray for a positive outcome," Mrs Mulligan said, a flash of anger flitting over her features. "I don't want that abusive prick anywhere near Siggy."

Oliver's heart thumped against his ribcage and his temper resurfaced. "Abusive? Ella never told me that either."

"Speculation isn't going to help at this point," Rafe said. "Let's get the tests done and wait for the results. If they're positive, then we can set up a meeting with a child psychologist and get a transition schedule in place. At her age, she may not need as much transition time as an older child would, but I'll leave that to the experts."

"And if the tests are negative?" Mrs Mulligan pressed. Ollie wanted to know the answer to that question too.

Sensible as ever, Rafe said, "We'll cross that bridge when we come to it."

20

Mia grinned when she heard Ollie enter the house, the tread of his work boots distinctive on the timber floorboards. But when she looked up from the box she was sifting through and saw his face, her grin slipped.

"Babe, what's wrong?"

He then laid out everything that had happened in Rafe's office plus his trip to the clinic for the DNA test, all while Mia sat curled in his lap and listened.

Because, honestly, what else could she do?

"If you want to rescind your offer to move in together, I get it," he said, looking utterly miserable.

Oliver was a protector through and through, so the thought he'd not done his duty by his own kid, that he hadn't protected her when she needed him most, was ripping him up inside. Mia could see it in his eyes, and in the way his shoulders slumped.

His heart was breaking.

She was not okay with that.

Tightening her grip on him, she said, "I'm not rescinding anything. You, my DILF, are stuck with me."

"DILF?"

"You know," she said, waggling her eyebrows. "Dad I'd Like to Fuck?"

She managed to pull a small smile out of him but it didn't last long. "But what if I'm not her dad?" he said, and pulled a photo of a little girl out of his shirt pocket.

From the way he was staring at that picture, Mia could tell he was already head-over-heels in love with her. And why wouldn't he be. Such a pretty little thing. Then she noticed something and took the picture, stared at it.

"She has my eyes," Ollie said, his voice gentle.

Mia really wanted to agree with him—the girl's eyes were identical to his—but she also didn't want to get his hopes up in case they were wrong.

That just seemed too cruel.

So instead, she said, "Babe, there's nothing we can do but wait."

"I know," he said.

She tucked the photo back in his pocket and snuggled against his broad chest. "Good thing you're a patient man."

Ollie snorted, a tiny smile lifting one corner of his mouth. "I know." Then he sighed and gestured to the box she'd been rifling through. "You've been busy."

Distraction. Yes. That's what they needed. "Charlie emailed me this morning with a quote for the renovations, so I was just looking for the photos Dad took when we first moved here."

"Oh?" His grin was back and one brow winged up in question. He knew as well as she did she was procrastinating.

"Yeah, okay, mostly I'm avoiding looking at my budget." She sighed and plucked at a loose thread on Oliver's sleeve. "Even with Charlie's family and friends discount, I can't afford all the work that needs doing. Charlie said it might actually be cheaper to pull the old girl down and start from scratch."

"What? That can't be right."

"The house is so old. Charlie said the underlying structural damage is more extensive than anticipated." Which explained why the bulk of the property value was in the land. The house was falling down. "He said we could salvage as much as possible and reuse it in the new build, but even so, it's going to cost a lot more than I'd budgeted for."

Oliver's arms tightened around her. "If we're going to do this thing, if we're going to be together and live together then we should split the costs too. You're not alone in this, Mia. I can help you cover what you need."

"No, you don't have to do that," Mia said, shaking her head as she sat up straight in his lap. "Besides, you need that money to build your forge. And I can get a bank loan for the amount I need."

"Sweetling, I can see the cogs turning in your head," Ollie said, his smile indulgent. "You're wondering how a thirty-five year old man who still lives at home could afford to help you, right?"

Was the man psychic? Or had she voiced her opinion out loud and not realised? Because that was *exactly* what she'd been thinking. How the hell was Oliver going to help her out financially when he couldn't even afford a place of his own?

She felt her cheeks heat and rolled her lips between her teeth, then ducked her gaze and said, "Maybe."

Oliver laughed. "I live at home because it's convenient, not because I can't afford to live anywhere else. You don't need a bank to loan you money, sweetling. I have more than enough for both of us." He slid his hand up to cup her breast. "Anyway, the interest I charge is much more fun."

Mia wriggled in his lap and felt the hardening bulge of his cock press against her hip. "I expect there'll be fees and charges to take into consideration too," she said, moaning as Ollie pressed his lips to her throat. The softness of his mouth, the heat of his breath was a sensual caress as he slowly worked his way into the V of her T-shirt. Lightly bit the swell of her breasts, scraping his teeth against her flesh and sending little bolts of arousal straight to her nipples.

And lower.

"Many, many fees. Lots of hidden charges," he murmured, tugging her T-shirt down to give him better access. Then he looked up and pinned her with that deliciously sinful gaze of his. "And I expect them to be paid as often as possible."

The next thing Mia knew, her lips were fused to Oliver's and they were tearing at each other's clothes. Shirts were discarded with speed and efficiency. Boots, jeans and underwear quickly followed. And then he was on top of her, kissing and licking and loving her on their makeshift bed of clothing.

He'd taken control away from her and she had to admit, she kinda liked it. Because as much as Oliver was willing to submit to her desires, as much as he needed her commanding touch, he was by no means a submissive man. And as much of a control freak as Mia was, she could appreciate a man who knew how to take charge, especially when pleasure was involved.

But when she felt his body about to enter hers, she pulled back. "Babe, you forgot the condom."

Oliver shook his head and his gaze met hers. "No, I didn't. I trust you, Mia."

Reaching up, she traced her fingers up the back of his neck and into his hair, fisted her hands in the dark-blond strands and gently tugged. "You sure?" she asked, knowing how big of a deal the decision was for him. She held her breath as she awaited his answer.

His hooded gaze and sexy, self-assured smile gave him away before his words did. "I love you, sweetling. I'm sure."

"Then what are you waiting for, Bennett?"

Ollie rocked his hips and nudged her pussy with the head of his cock before pulling back then nudging her again, teasing her with everything he knew she wanted. She growled in frustration. He grinned in return. "I'm waiting for my lady to tell me she loves me too."

Mia stared at Oliver, at the openness in his expression, the desire in his eyes, and let her emotions overtake her. Her usual instinct to hide her smile, to restrain her joy and hold herself above such small concerns melted away to nothing.

Her love for the man staring down at her, the man patiently waiting for her to get her shit together and confirm what he already knew, was anything but small.

With a broad smile she said, "I love you, Ollie. I'm sure too." Then she tightened her grip in his hair, tugged him close enough for their lips to touch and took back control. "Now hurry up and fuck me."

His tongue slid between her lips at the same time his cock slid deep inside her body, and if she'd thought sex with Oliver was great before, it was nothing compared to the feeling of having absolutely nothing between them. Feeling his skin on hers, absorbing his heat, revelling in his need for her as he thrust deep and hard.

"Yes... Ollie!"

"Yes, love," he whispered in her ear. "Tell me what you want."

"You," she cried out, clutching him to her, wrapping her arms around his powerful body, entwining her legs with his. Holding on as he drove her to the edge of orgasm. "I want you. I want everything that comes with wanting you. I want a life with you, babies with you, everything with you. I want everything, Ollie. You're my everything."

He smiled down at her, his gaze reflecting the love she felt down to her very soul. "Sweetling," he murmured, brushing his lips over hers, and with the next thrust of his hips, Mia's orgasm exploded into being, shattering her into a million pieces of well satiated woman.

Oliver's own release followed with a masculine grunt of satisfaction. "Fuck," he groaned, collapsing on top of her before rolling to her side and gathering her close. "That was incredible. You're incredible," he said, nuzzling her temple. Then she felt his lips curve up in a smile. "And you're my everything too, Mia. I can't wait to start a family with you."

"Really?" she said, dragging the word out while propping herself up on her elbow so she could watch Ollie's face.

He tucked one arm under his head and grinned back at her. "Really, really."

"So if I were to tell you," Mia began, drawing lazy circles on Oliver's chest, "that my birth control pills run out next week, you'd be okay with that...?"

Ollie's chest bounced, his chuckle deep and sinister as he grabbed her hand and moved it to cup his already harding cock. "What do you think?"

Mia straddled his big body and raked her fingernails down his abs, delighted in the way the muscles tensed and flexed. Gloried in the lust reflected in his gorgeous eyes. "I think practice makes perfect."

21

The next couple of days passed easily enough. Ollie moved Mia into The Forge indefinitely, and she organised for the contents of Someday to go into storage. Ollie finished Mrs Williams's fugly flamingo gates, and Mia readied the yard for the wedding photos by weeding the pathways and mowing the grass.

Their days were filled with work, but their nights were filled with copious amounts of fucking. Mia lost count of the orgasms she'd had. Not that she was complaining. Her pussy had never been so well used, and by such a gifted lover. But it seemed admitting to wanting to have his baby had sent Oliver into a frenzy, and he'd taken it as a personal challenge to knock her up as soon as humanly possible.

Mia was exhausted, but in the best way.

She couldn't remember the last time she'd smiled so much.

By Friday morning everything was on track for Toby and Lucy's wedding the following day. The Bennett family had descended on Melville's Cross en masse, overtaking The Forge and making Mia very glad she had Ollie's room to retreat to when it all got to be too much. Jane and Mary Melville were holed up in the patisserie preparing the wedding cake and other desserts. And Jess, the biological mother of Charlie's twin daughters, was putting the finishing touches on Lucy's dress.

Everything had been planned down to the last detail, so of course something went wrong at the last minute.

Like a comedy of errors, anything that could have gone wrong did. Such as the chapel administrator calling on Friday night to apologise, saying the chapel had been double booked for Saturday afternoon and under their 'first in, best dressed' rules, Toby and Lucy needed to find somewhere else to get hitched.

Then Jane had called to say the oven at the patisserie had broken down and the wedding cake was ruined, so the ready-to-pop pregnant lady and her mother were working on a solution there.

And then on Saturday morning, when the pure white roses and other assorted flowers Toby had ordered for the bouquets and table arrangements showed up, they were various shades of pink.

Chaos reigned. The bride was near to tears, the groom looked ready to murder someone for making his woman cry, and everyone else stood around arguing, no closer to figuring out what the hell they were going to do.

But Mia leaned into the situation like she'd been

born to it. She'd been making chaos her bitch for close to two decades, and she wasn't about to stop now. Especially if it meant using her powers for good and helping her family.

Because that's what the Bennetts were to her now.

Family.

Standing in the kitchen, where most of the family had gathered for breakfast, she said, "Can I have everyone's attention, please?"

When the noise didn't quieten down she looked at Oliver. His deep voice boomed out of him as he simply said, "Oi! Listen up."

"Thanks, babe. If I could just interject for a moment," she said, holding up a tablet, "But I have a plan."

After they'd received the news about the chapel, Mia had made some calls. A lot of people owed her a lot of favours and she couldn't think of a better time to call in their chits.

It was also a stroke of luck that she just happened to own a house with a huge backyard and the best views in town.

"I have troops incoming with marquees, tables and seating. We can set up everything at Someday. I mean, we already cleaned up the yard for the photos anyway so we may as well put it to good use. Rafe?"

"Yes?"

"Can you call the caterers, the band and the celebrant and let them know about the change of venue? Then check on Jane and the cake?"

"On it," he said, shoving a piece of toast in his mouth.

"Toby?"

The big man didn't answer, just stared at her with one brow raised and a look of displeasure on his face.

"Are you sure you can't use those?" she asked, pointing to the hot pink roses piled up on the kitchen bench.

"Positive," he said through gritted teeth.

Mia nodded. "Then I want you and your brothers—not Crispin—to visit every resident in town who has white flowers growing in their yard and use your considerable Bennett charm to beg, borrow, steal or swap them for those pink ones. I suggest starting with Mayor Rose and working your way down from there."

The tension eased from Toby's features and he half-smiled as he tucked Lucy under his arm. "Yeah, we can do that."

"And what will I be doing?" Crispin spoke up from his spot at the kitchen table.

Grinning at the handsome interior designer, she said, "You're coming with me to Someday. I need someone with your expertise to tell my soldiers where to set up the marquees to make the most of the space and the views."

Cris threw out a mock salute. "Lead the way."

"Uly?"

"Yes, sweetheart?" The old flirt's eyes practically twinkled with mischief.

"I need you to source as many boxes of white fairy lights as you can and bring them to Someday in two hours or less."

The Bennett family patriarch smiled broadly. "I like a woman who knows what she wants. Consider it done."

Mia nodded her thanks. "Everyone else needs to help Lucy and her bridesmaids get ready, including getting to their beauty appointments on time, starting with their mani-pedis in forty-five minutes." She tucked her tablet under her arm. "Everyone know what they're doing?"

Everyone just sort of murmured, shrugged and half-nodded, their lack of urgency causing Major Mia's back to straighten, her chin to lift and her voice to snap out, "I said does everyone know what they're doing?"

A roomful of startled people blurted out, "Yes."

"Good. Then let's get moving."

A few hours later, her troops, led by a very competent corporal and guided by a very commanding Crispin, had assembled white marquees for the ceremony and dinner, dressed the chairs, set the tables, filled the trees with Ulysses's fairy lights, and helped Toby dress the entire area with so many white and pale pink flowers that her backyard looked magical. Beautiful.

To top things off, the band had arrived on time, the smell from the caterer's trucks was simply divine, and Jane's solution to the wedding cake problem was perfection.

"Thank you, Mia," Toby said quietly, giving her a hug. "You saved the day."

"You're very welcome," she replied, then gasped as another pair of arms came around her, sandwiching her between them and the groom.

"I don't know how you pulled this off, Mia, but

Toby's right," Charlie said, the sincerity in his voice throwing her off. She still didn't trust him not to put a frog in her handbag or something equally childish. "Thank you."

Mia shrugged. "I worked in logistics, guys. Organising other people and telling them where to go was literally my job. Which reminds me, I had Uly put your clothes upstairs so you could shower and get dressed here."

Both twins kissed her cheeks then disappeared up the front stairs and into the old house.

After checking her watch, Mia went over her checklist one last time then grabbed the walkie-talkie from her back pocket. "Sixty minutes and counting everyone." After she received the appropriate responses, she handed the walkie and the tablet to the corporal. "You know what to do?"

He raised one brow and grinned at her. "Don't fuck it up?"

"I knew there was a reason I like you, Perkins."

"Should we synchronise our watches," he teased.

Mia mirrored his expression. "I'll synchronise my foot up your arse if you fuck this up."

"Yes, Ma'am."

Crispin appeared at her elbow, swinging his car keys around his finger. "You ready to go?"

With one final scan of the yard, she nodded. "Let's get out of here."

Mia needed to get ready. More importantly, she needed to check on Ollie. Her man had skulked off earlier than his brothers, claiming he needed more time than them to get ready, something about his hair. She'd grinned and waved him off, but she'd seen the underlying tension in his posture. The worry he'd tried so hard to hide all week.

The man she loved was hurting, and as much as Mia wished she could do more for him, could give him what he needed, she knew it was out of her hands. Because what he really needed were the results of that bloody paternity test and he needed them yesterday. But there was nothing she could do to get them. She'd tried. Rafe had tried. But apparently it was going to take as long as it took.

No cutting ahead.

No rush jobs.

Just time.

And for someone like Mia who preferred action over doing nothing, waiting for other people to do their job was intensely frustrating.

I hate waiting.

22

Ollie stared at his reflection in the mirror and barely recognised himself. A haircut had seemed like a good idea at the time, but he probably should have thought better of doing it himself. Still, he liked the shorter style better than he'd thought he would, even if he looked a bit scruffy.

Setting to work on his beard, he made sure to leave enough stubble to appease Mia's newfound fascination with it. Especially when he had his head between her thighs.

He knew she'd been keeping him busy all week, distracting him with sex and odd jobs so he wouldn't think about other things—paternity test things—but thoughts of Sigrid were never far from his mind.

If Sigrid was his, as he believed she was, why hadn't Ella told him about her? He could have helped out, he would have wanted to be a part of his daughter's life. But maybe that was the problem. Ella didn't want a man in her life, complicating things. And if Ollie had known about Sigrid, he would have insisted on being in her life. So maybe it was better that he hadn't been there?

He shook his head, not believing that for a second.

He may have had a shitty mother, but he had an awesome father. Ulysses Bennett was always there when his kids needed him. No matter what he was doing, where he was doing it or who he was doing it with, if one of his children needed him, he was there.

No questions asked.

No doubt about it.

That's what Ollie wanted with Sigrid. To make her that same promise. If only he got the chance.

And he really wanted that chance.

A knock on the bathroom door snapped him out of his thoughts.

"Ollie? It's just me, babe."

The sound of Mia's voice soothed his nerves, until he wondered what she'd think of his hair. Hesitantly, he called out, "Come in."

"I just wanted to check—holy shit!" Wide eyes met his in the mirror. "Where's your hair?"

He smirked at the instant heat that flashed in her eyes and cocked one brow. "You don't like it?" he teased, feeling much more confident at her reaction.

"I fucking love it," she murmured as she moved closer. Reaching up, she slid her fingers through his shortened locks and made a fist, made him growl. "You look... So. Damn. Hot." She nodded absently as though agreeing with herself. "I really think we need to have sex now."

He couldn't resist messing with her. "We *need* to?"

"Yes. Right now."

"Good thing I'm already naked then." Ollie smirked, his cock jerking to life at the very mention of sex with his goddess. "But what about you?"

"Give me ten seconds."

Ollie made a point of counting down those seconds, chuckling when she was completely naked by the count of seven. As a reward, he slipped two fingers deep inside her tight, wet cunt. Clinging to his arms, Mia did her valiant best not to collapse on the floor, her knees threatening to give way as he easily brought her to orgasm.

Sexy things Ollie had discovered about Major Mia in the past week #147: she loved a good finger-bang and came so damn hard and fast she gushed all over his hand.

He fucking loved it.

His dirty girl.

Mia's fingers curled into his biceps, scoring him with her nails, making him moan as she screamed, "Ollie, fuck, fuck, yes, fuck!"

"That dirty mouth of yours needs to be put to better use, sweetling," he said as she clung to him.

But he knew if she went down on her knees, she'd be in pain for the rest of the afternoon and evening, and he wouldn't have her missing out on the fun of the wedding just because he wanted his cock sucked. So instead, he lifted her body and wrapped her legs around his waist, then walked into the shower and turned on the taps.

As they waited for the water to heat, he nibbled a path up her neck to her mouth, then slipped his tongue between her lips and stole her breath with his kiss.

Put her dirty mouth to a much better use.

Ollie kissed her slowly, passionately. Licked inside her mouth and sucked on her tongue until he felt her melt in his arms.

"Ollie, yes." Staring at him with complete trust in her lovely blue gaze, Mia nodded, and Ollie thrust his hips and slid deep inside his lover.

Digging his fingers into her arse to hold her up, he made love to her with long, languid strokes of his cock, lost himself in the pleasure of her body wrapped around his like a fist. Relished the rush of sensation he'd denied himself for a lifetime.

Being inside Mia without the condom to dull his senses was fucking amazing. Her pussy felt like silk, hot, molten silk. He felt every ripple of her muscles, every flutter, every quiver. He felt *her*, and she felt so fucking good.

When Mia's orgasm hit, Ollie felt her body latch around his cock and squeeze the ever-loving life out of him, and he knew he was never going back.

His old life was done. Finished. No more one night stands, no more hook-ups, no more booty-calls. He had everything he wanted right here in his arms.

Unexpected.

Inevitable.

Perfect.

And he was no longer envious of his siblings. Ollie finally had what they did.

Something permanent, something meaningful.

Something real.

Ollie was lost to this woman. Lost to his love for her, his trust in her. No one else would ever hold a candle to her.

Mia was his first and she would be his last.

As it always should have been.

Managing to hold his orgasm in check just long enough to send Mia over the edge first, he murmured, "I love you," against her cheek, then came inside her, thrusting until the last of his come was spent.

Mia rested her head on his shoulder, her breaths coming hard and fast against his neck until she lifted her face to his and pressed the sweetest kiss to his mouth.

"I love you, too."

When she laid her head on his shoulder again, he asked, "Will you marry me?"

Jerking her head up again, her face was the perfect picture of surprise. "Really?"

"Really, really." He stroked her hair away from her face and stared into her lovely eyes. "No matter what happens from here on out, I only need you to know one thing."

"What's that?"

"If you ever run away again, I will hunt your stubborn arse down. I need you in my life, sweetling. I want you in my life. Not just as my lover, but my best friend too." He carried her under the water and set her on her feet. "Say you'll marry me, Emilia. Say you'll be my wife, you'll have my babies." He took a breath. "Say you'll be mine."

Reaching up to run her fingers through his shortened hair, she smiled and nodded and whispered, "Yes."

"Are you nervous?"

Ollie ignored Rafe's stupid question and focussed on his breathing exercises, and when that didn't help settle his nerves, he grabbed Mia's hand and laced their fingers together, anchored himself in the moment with her.

"I'm about to meet my daughter for the first time. Of course I'm fucking nervous."

The results of the paternity test had finally arrived on the Thursday following Toby and Lucy's wedding.

And it was positive.

Oliver Bennett was a father.

Rafe had immediately consulted with a child psychologist and they'd worked out a visitation and transition schedule with Ella's parents. Three weeks had passed since Oliver had discovered his daughter's existence, and this was to be the first of several shorter visits to get Sigrid used to Ollie and Mia, and for them to get used to her.

"Language," Mia scolded softly, though there was an undertone of humour in the command. "You're going to have to cut back on the swearing for a while."

"You can talk," he replied. "You swear like a soldier."

Mia chuckled. "I was a soldier."

"Yes. Was. What's your new excuse?"

She squeezed his hand tightly. "Don't be peevish. Take deep breaths. And babe," she said, staring up at him, "you've got this."

Oliver took a deep breath then slowly let it out. Then he took another, and another. And then another thought struck him and his breath stuck in his lungs again as his nerves twisted tighter. "What if she doesn't like me?"

Charlie appeared beside him. "Impossible, little brother. Sigrid is going to adore you."

"Just don't forget," Rafe said in that irritating I'm-a-lawyer-and-I-know-everything tone, "this is just the first step in the process, little more than an introduction. Once she learns who you are, learns to trust you and—"

"Oh, enough," Mia snapped. "Back off, the pair of you. It's going to be overwhelming enough as it is for both Ollie and Sigrid without the whole Bennett clan crowding around them. Now everybody get back inside and stay there."

Ollie rolled his lips between his teeth to stop himself from laughing at his brothers, then winked at Mia.

My protector.

Her scolding sent everyone scuttling back inside the house, grumbling the whole way about "bossy women".

Once he saw Charlie, Rafe and the rest of them had done as they were told, and left him alone, he relaxed a little.

But when the Mulligans pulled up in front of The Forge and helped a little girl out of the car, his nerves kicked him in the gut and knocked the wind out of him.

Mr and Mrs Mulligan smiled as they led their grand-daughter around the car to the garden gate. "What a lovely garden. Look Siggy, can you see the butterflies in the garden?"

Sigrid stood half-hidden behind her grandparents, using them as her shield, and Ollie understood. This wasn't going to be easy. For any of them.

But it was going to be worth it.

Kneeling down so he was closer to her eye level, he said, "Do you know who I am?"

Sigrid nodded. "You're my daddy."

Daddy. The word made tears, hot and sudden spring to Ollie's eyes. "That's right, sweetling. I'm your daddy."

"Mummy said you're a Viking," she said, her voice quiet and shy as she hugged her grandfather's leg like a life-buoy. "Is that true?"

Apparently Ella had shown their daughter photographs of him, told her fantastical stories about why he was never there with them, there for her, including that he was a Viking off on a tremendous adventure.

He didn't want to shatter any trust she still held in her mother, but he wouldn't enforce the lie either.

"Well, I'm half Viking. My mother is from Norway, land of the Vikings. Do you know where Norway is?"

Eyes the exact same shade of blue as his peered up at him, and sandy-blonde curls like her mother's bobbed around her face as she shook her head. "No."

Ollie smiled at her bluntness. "That's okay. Maybe when you're older we can go there together, go an adventure and visit the real Vikings. Would you like that?"

Sigrid looked up at her grandfather who smiled and gave her an encouraging nod. "Okay," she said.

"Would you like to come inside and meet your cousins? Josie and Diana made a special doll just for you. Do you like dolls?"

"She loves dolls, don't you Siggy?" Her grandmother held her hand out and waited patiently for Sigrid to take it. "Let's go inside and meet everybody, okay?"

The little girl dug the toe of her shoe into the ground. "Is there cake?"

"Siggy," her grandmother started scolding her, but Ollie chuckled.

"Yes, love. There's always cake in this house."

That earned him a shy smile. "Okay."

The Mulligans led Sigrid up the veranda steps while Ollie and Mia hung back for a moment.

"Are you okay?" she asked quietly as Ollie levered to his feet.

He nodded, even as silent tears leaked down his face. "I didn't think it was possible to love someone I've never met before, so much." Ollie wiped his eyes on his sleeve, then whispered, "She's so beautiful."

Mia took his hand and walked towards the house. "You're a good man, Oliver Bennett," she said, stroking his tattooed forearm, the one he'd added a new set of runes to the same day he'd found out she was his: Sigrid. In blue ink.

When they reached the front door of the house, he shook his head, and said, "I have a daughter. Me. The second biggest womaniser in the family and I have a daughter. Dad's right. It's karma."

Mia snorted. "You're no womaniser. A bit of a slut, perhaps, but I find it hard to believe you ever seduced someone without them knowing exactly what they were getting in return."

He wrapped his arms around her. "Why are you so good to me?"

"Because you're good to me," she said, planting a quick kiss on his lips. "And speaking of daughters, how do you feel about having another one?"

Mia's question caught him off guard, but when Oliver pulled back to look at her, he couldn't contain the grin spreading across his face.

"I feel pretty good about it, actually," he said. "Why? Are you trying to tell me something?" he added playfully.

"Hardly. It's much too early for that."

Ollie dropped his hands to Mia's belly and lowered his voice. "You stopped taking your pill weeks ago," he reminded her. "It only takes once, sweetling, and with the amount of sex we've been having, I'd say our chances are better than most."

"We'll see," she said. "But right now you have to go in there and teach that little girl what it means to be a Bennett."

His brow furrowed as he absorbed her words. "You'll be a Bennett soon. What does it mean to you?"

His lover slid her hands over his chest and straightened his shirt collar. "Laughter, kindness, love,"—she smiled up at him—"and acceptance. Knowing you love me for who I am, that you accept me, every part of me without question, that's what's important." Then she winked. "And hugs. Lots of hugs."

Yanking Mia into his arms, Ollie hugged her tightly, only releasing the breath he'd been holding when he felt her hug him back. "Thank you, Mia. I couldn't do this without you."

"Sure you could."

"Fine. I don't want to do this without you." He cupped her cheeks and brushed his lips over hers one final time, willed her to feel his love for her in the gentle caress, then took her hand in his, relaxed when he felt her reassuring squeeze. "Let's go meet our daughter."

EPILOGUE TWO

T*he Abbey Medieval Tournament, July, two years later.*

Sweat poured down Oliver's back and face as he pounded the hot metal into shape. Making arrowheads was fucking tedious work but they were quick enough to bang out for the audience and gave him something to sell to the other re-enactors later.

He was also acutely aware of Mia watching him from the shade of their tent, running her lustful gaze over his half-naked body. Did he preen under her potent stare, maybe flex his muscles a little more than necessary for the job he was doing?

Yes.

Absofuckinglutely yes.

And if it wasn't for the audience of fifty or more

people milling around watching him as his sister narrated the demonstration, he would have thrown down his tools, picked up his wife and been balls deep in her luscious warmth before they'd even found their bed.

It was a distracting thought, one his brain refused to let go of, which made his job—and his cock—harder than anticipated.

Glancing up, he caught the direction of Mia's gaze. It seemed she'd noticed his dilemma too, and when she lifted her eyes to his he couldn't help but grin at her. When she sank her teeth into her bottom lip then slowly released it, teased him with the knowledge of what those teeth could do to his body, his cock twitched again and he had to suppress a groan of need.

Soon, sweetling. Soon....

"Blacksmithing is one of those rare occupations where the tools of our trade have not changed for thousands of years," Abby told the crowd. "As you can see by the way my brother—"

"So you're not married then?" a female voice called out from the midst of the onlookers, cutting Abby off.

Ollie huffed out a laugh and shook his head and his sister's lips pinched in a look he knew well. She was trying not to laugh. "To him?" she said, thumbing over her shoulder in Ollie's direction. "No, we're not married."

"Best news I've heard all day," a different woman called out, followed by the twittering laughter and chuckles of others.

"Our resident shield maiden, on the other hand," Abby continued, indicating Mia, "*is* married to him, and trust me when I say you do not want to piss off a Viking bride."

Oliver watched Mia step from the shadows of their tent, her kohl-rimmed eyes narrowed and her favourite battle-axe in her hands. She looked glorious, a true warrior maiden dressed to kill with a studded leather breastplate buckled over her tunic, carved leather vambraces strapped to her forearms and her long, dark hair braided into a fauxhawk.

Picking up the whetstone Ollie kept close at hand, Mia began sharpening the axe with slow, threatening strokes. The rasp of the stone on the metal blade caused some members of the audience to shuffle their feet, suddenly nervous, until someone called out, "Is it true a wife was allowed to cut off her cheating husbands junk?"

Ollie chuckled at that old chestnut.

"Unfortunately no," Abby said, with a twist of her lips. "Even the lowliest of men were allowed concubines and sex slaves, if they could afford them." Then she grinned. "But can you imagine if it was true? I mean, nothing says 'keep it in your pants' like a dick nailed to the wall."

As the audience burst into laughter, Mia chose that exact moment to slam the blade of the axe into the large wooden stump by her feet. The blade made a heavy *thunk* sound as it bit into the wood and the audience jumped, then laughed again, only in that nervous way people do after a good scare: part on edge, part relieved, and a quick check of their pants to make sure they didn't just piss themselves.

Mia folded her arms over her chest and sniffed, malevolent disdain written across her pretty features as she scanned the crowd, almost daring the women who'd called out to try and take what was hers.

Like she had anything to worry about.

His man-whoring days were well and truly done the second she'd come back into his life.

Ollie's gaze locked with Mia's and his heartbeat ratcheted up several notches. The lust he saw reflected in her lovely eyes made his dick harden even more, and his need to end the fucking demonstration so he could act on that lust had him slamming his hammer against the anvil with swift precision.

Again he thanked the gods for Abby, who quickly picked up on his change of pace and mood. "I think we've gotten a little off track," she said, then continued with her rehearsed spiel about the history of black-smithing and Viking culture.

Half an hour later, the demo was done, the crowd had moved off to investigate the next exhibition of medieval life, and Ollie went in search of his wife, his mind overflowing with all the wicked things he wanted to do to her.

He didn't have to go far. Mia had retreated inside their spacious tent and he found her unfastening her belt and casting it and the assortment of accoutrements attached to it aside.

Ollie slowed his steps as he entered the tent, better to appreciate the view as his wife unfastened the rest of her leather armour and added it to the pile by her feet.

"Where's Abby?" Mia asked, distracted by the one buckle on her vambrace that always got stuck.

Ollie knew he should probably fix it, but then he wouldn't be able to do what he did next. "My favourite sister," he began, taking her forearm in his hands and working the buckle free. Any excuse to touch her.

"She's your only sister," Mia reminded him, chuckling.

Ollie grinned as he tugged the last strap free. "My favourite sister has agreed to give us some alone time. She and Wolf are keeping the girls with them until after the jousting exhibition, so that gives us about an hour before they get back."

During the demonstration, Abby's husband had been put in charge of his nieces. The big man was currently Sigrid's favourite person due to the fact he allowed her to colour in his plethora of tattoos, which made him the perfect babysitter. He'd taken Ollie's now five-year-old daughter and her one-year-old sister, Brenna, to the petting zoo, and would now be meeting up with Abby for lunch and jousting.

"Hmm, you sure that'll be enough time?" Mia said, untying the sides of her apron dress.

Sliding his hands over her hips, Ollie pulled Mia against his body, pressed his hard cock between her thighs. Tracked her tongue as she swiped it over her bottom lip. "It's never enough time with you, sweetling." Then he bent his head to kiss her but she shoved him away.

"You're all sweaty," she said, laughing. "You stink."

"But it's a manly stink," he replied, winking as he struck a pose and flexed his muscles for her.

"Ugh, manly or not, you need a wash, so why don't you get some hot water and I'll grab the soap."

The stern look on Mia's face told him it wasn't a suggestion, and that just made his dick jerk against his trousers, eager to obey so they could get on with it.

Ducking outside again, he filled a jug with the water they kept in a pot near the fire, then returned and emptied the jug into the metal basin Mia had placed on the table.

She closed the heavy tent flaps and tied them shut, giving them privacy, and the flickering of a lantern gave them light to see by.

"Strip," she commanded.

Ollie wasted no time complying with her wishes, sitting down to remove his boots, leg wraps and trousers in record time, then stood and helped Mia remove her tunic dress. It was a little tighter than the last time she'd worn it, her baby bump swelling her waistline several inches now, not to mention her breasts.

She didn't need that push-up bra anymore. Breast-feeding Brenna had caused her tits to grow two sizes larger, and her new pregnancy was making them tender in a way Ollie loved putting to good use.

As soon as they were both naked, Mia soaked a cloth in the warm water, then rubbed soap on it and washed Oliver's body. They bathed together all the time at home, but there was something so much more erotic about doing it like this. Facing each other, completely bare to each other without even a curtain of water to hide behind.

Her strokes with the cloth were firm and efficient, up and over his chest, his shoulders, down his back and over his arse. She wiped away the grime from his hands and the sweat from his face and neck, and she took particular care of his inner thighs and rampant erection.

But not the type of care Ollie craved from her.

"Mia," he groaned, reaching for her again. "Sweetling, please. I need to be inside you."

She tossed the cloth into the basin. "Get on the bed and wait for me," she ordered. "On your back."

Ollie smirked. His wife's need was just as great as his if her underlying tone of urgency was anything to go by.

A pregnant Mia was a horny Mia.

Once he was on his back on their very big, comfortable Viking bed, Mia joined him, straddled him. Bending forwards, she licked and kissed a path starting in the hollow at his throat and ending on his lips, where she slipped her tongue inside his mouth and kissed him long and deep.

He speared his fingers into her hair and angled her head to give him better access to her, to deepen their kiss further. Mia rubbed her body against his, the electric sensation of her hard nipples and wet pussy stroking his heated flesh made all the more erotic by her sultry moans of pleasure.

"Fuck, baby," she whimpered, reaching between them to fist her hand around his dick. "I need you."

A moment later he was sheathed inside Mia's tight, wet pussy.

Her head lolled back and her mouth fell open but when she rocked her hips, when she pressed herself down on him until he couldn't get any deeper inside her, she locked her gaze with his. Bored into his very soul. "Fuck me," she demanded.

Ollie gripped Mia's thighs so tightly her flesh spilled out from between his fingers. Her body wasn't as toned as it used to be, before Brenna was born. She was softer now, fuller, bore the marks of childbirth in her stretch-marks and the scar from her C-section.

Mia Bennett was the most beautiful woman Oliver had ever known. And he was the luckiest sonofabitch in the world to have made her his.

He bucked his hips as he gripped her thighs, pulling her down as he thrust up. Mia cried out before shoving her fist in her mouth and biting down, silencing herself and making Ollie chuckle. If anyone passing by were paying close enough attention, the sound of their bed shifting, creaking in that telltale rhythmic way that all beds did, would give away their purpose in a heartbeat. Mia jamming her fist in her mouth in the hopes of disguising their fucking as something else was adorable.

"I love you," Ollie growled.

Reaching up, he hooked one hand around her neck and pulled his lover down for another kiss.

"I love you, too," Mia murmured against his mouth, then attacked him with a vigour that matched their thrusting hips.

Ollie felt Mia's pussy tighten, felt her silky heat clamping and releasing his dick, tighter and tighter. She was close. So fucking close. And so was he.

Need gripped his spine and his balls drew up tight. Shifting one hand from her hips, he stroked her swollen clit with the roughened pad of his thumb.

"Baby, yes," she moaned. "Fuck yes!"

Then she doubled down and lifted her body off his, let his cock slip from inside her just enough that she could squeeze it with her cunt as she slammed herself down again, all while he rubbed her clit and swore under his breath. He was ready to explode.

"Sweetling, I can't hold back much longer."

"Then don't," she said, then threw back her head and screamed as her body tightened around his.

Ollie's own orgasm followed quickly and he thrust his hips so hard he lifted them both off the bed, his back arching as spasm after spasm shot through his dick, filling Mia's sweet pussy with his come.

When they came back down to earth, he gathered her close, pressed a kiss to her forehead and stroked his hand over her belly.

"Are you okay?" he whispered, continuing to press kisses to her face and mouth. "Any pain in your back or hip?"

Mia chuckled and snuggled closer, played with the beads braided into his beard. "Are you worried about me, or asking if I'm ready for round two?"

He cocked one brow and grinned. "Can't it be both?"

His wife poked him in his ribs which in turn led to a tickling match which in turn led to round two.

That night as they lay in bed, their daughters curled up between them, Ollie reached over and brushed a lock of hair from Mia's cheek. His wife was sleeping soundly. Growing a baby was tiring. "I love you," he whispered again.

"I love you, too, Daddy," Sigrid whispered back, making him chuckle. She was supposed to be asleep.

"Me, three," Mia added, blinking her eyes open to stare at him. Eyes that reflected all the love and devotion he never knew he was capable of giving, never knew he needed until Mia fell out of and then stumbled back into his life.

An amazing wife, two beautiful daughters and another baby on the way.

He really was the luckiest sonofabitch around.

THE END

MORE FROM JENNIE KEW

The Bennett's Bastards Series

Third Time Lucky

This Time Around

His Own Heaven

The Viking Blues

Size Doesn't Matter

Bennett's Bastards #6 (TBA)

Bennett's Bastards #7 (TBA)

The Brisbane Bachelors Series

The Book Shop Girl and The Billionaire

The Roller Derby Darling and The Delinquent

The Boss Babe CEO and The Scoundrel (2024)

Audiobooks

The Book Shop Girl and The Billionaire

The Q Collection

No Rest For The Wicked

I Saw, I Conquered, I Came

Pushing Rope

Dirty Laundry

Santa Claus Is Coming

Carved In Stone

Battery Operated Boyfriend

Tying The Knot

Quirky: The Complete Q Collection

ACKNOWLEDGEMENTS

To my family for all their encouragement, their love and understanding, thank you for being you and for putting up with me being me, especially when deadlines are involved.

A special thank you to my crit partners, my cheer squad, my sisters-in-arms, Bec McMaster and Kylie Griffin. You always challenge me to be a better writer and I really couldn't do this without you. Thank you for keeping me sane...*ish*.

To my editor, Kristin Scearce, who accepts my weird writing style and quirky humour as canon and is still willing to work with me, you rock!

And finally to my readers, thank you for taking this journey with me, and for allowing me to share with you all the people and places who occupy my head and my heart. I hope you enjoy reading about them as much as I enjoy writing about them.

MEET THE AUTHOR

Jennie has always enjoyed reading but never had aspirations of becoming a published author. At least not until a dance with death made her ask herself what she really wanted out of life, and she's been writing ever since.

When not writing stories about her imaginary friends, Jennie can usually be found reading a book, watching a movie or building stuff out of Lego. She lives in regional New South Wales with her husband, her husband's magnificent beard, and their small menagerie of furry companions.

www.jenniekew.com

GLOSSARY

As all of my books are set in Australia and use a lot of Australian terms and slang, I've created this guide for my readers to keep you on track when you come across any Aussie-isms in my books.

A bit of all right: If someone is 'a bit of all right' they're considered to be very attractive.

Ambo: Short for ambulance, the term has come to mean anyone associated with any of the public or private ambulance services, their drivers and paramedics.

Arse: Aussie spelling of ass, aka buttocks, bottom, booty and bum.

Arvo and *Sarvo*: 'Afternoon' and 'this afternoon'.

Copper: Police, cops.

Cricket nets: batting practice cages for the Australian summer sport of cricket.

Fashion Rag/Local Rag: Fashion magazine, any locally produced magazines or newspapers.

Fierie/s: Firefighter/s.

Fivesies: Pre-dinner drinks and snacks, usually consisting of wine, and cheese, served around 5 p.m.

Fuck-knuckle: An idiot.

G'day: Pronounced 'gidday', this official Australian greeting is a contraction of the words 'good' and 'day'.

G-string: Thong underwear

Kiwi: Pronounced 'kee-wee', anyone born in New Zealand.

Larrikin: An unruly, boisterous but generally good natured person, usually male.

Mate: Unlike paranormal or sci-fi erotic romances where your 'mate' is the person you're fated to be with for the rest of your life, in Australian culture 'mate' could mean anyone from your best friend to some random bloke you just met.

Pav: Pavlova, a dessert made from baked meringue, topped with cream and fresh fruit, particularly popular around Christmas. We nicked it from the Kiwis.

Phwoar: An estimation of the sound one makes when a bit of all right enters your vicinity. See also, 'panting' and 'drooling'.

RFS: Rural Fire Service.

Sanga: Sandwich.

She'll be right, mate: Usually given as a response when someone is offering aid of some kind, it means 'Everything will be fine but thanks for asking'.

Thongs: Flip-flops/footwear

Togs: A swimsuit.

Tradie: Any tradesman.

Uni: Pronounced 'you-nee', University aka College.

Yeah, nah and *Nah, yeah*: Whichever word the phrase ends on, is the affirmative answer, therefore 'Yeah, nah' means 'No', and 'Nah, yeah' means 'Yes'.